VM L

THE BETRAYED

LARSSON MEDIA

Also by VM Larsson

The Friland Murders Series

The Alibi
The Betrayed
The Clover

True Crime Scandinavia
- Short Stories -

A Deadly Night
Fatal Flames
See Her Dead
Deadly Encore
Dance of Betrayal

THE BETRAYED: THE FRILAND MURDERS BOOK 2

ISBN: 978-91-989200-1-7
Cover: The Cover Collection
vmlarsson.com

The Friland Islands are a fictional group of Swedish islands in the North Sea, originating from early Norse settlements southwest of Norway. Friland consists of 288 islands; only six are inhabited: Friland, Fossa, Breda, Vidare, Holm, and Lunna.

The old Norse dialect known as Frilandic is spoken. You can look up the location at coordinates 57.108233, and 4.789287. For a detailed map of the Friland Islands and their exact location, head to vmlarsson.com.

List of characters

Moa Bakke – Forensic Technician and a **main character**.
Fredrik Dal – Detective Inspector and a **main character**.
Ylva Moore – Detective Inspector.
Erik Storm – Forensic Technician and Moa's colleague.
Anna Vall – Prosecutor and works closely with the police team.
Grim Mattis – Digital Forensic Technician.
Ida Steen – Forensic Pathologist.
Jake Lund – Lawyer and entrepreneur.
Sven Stark – Security Officer. | **Rune Ek** – Entrepreneur.
Tore Vikholm – A drunken sailor.
Hanna – Owner of The Norse Inn.
Ingrid – Works at The Norse Inn.
Lars Gaard – Owner of The Nordic Crust Pizza.
Benny Palm – Photographer. | **Claire** – Benny's sister.
Vera – Moa's mother. | **Tomas** – Moa's brother.
Kajsa – Personal assistant. | **Nora** – A trusted hairdresser.
Vilda – A private investigator.

PROLOGUE

THE ICY BREATH of the February night paints frost flowers across the windshield, delicate yet deceptive. In the driver's seat, a man drifts into a light sleep, gently rocked by the boat's sway.

The transponder goes dark. A hand signals the all-clear, and metal meets water. The man jerks awake too late. The sea swallows him swiftly, leaving only a faint ripple on the surface, as if nothing had happened.

CHAPTER ONE
November

MOA BAKKE STARED at the North Sea, its waves crashing furiously against the cliffs below. Merely a few steps for ward, she would have seconds left to live. She had been to this precipice by the lighthouse before, but never this close to the edge. In the distance, the faint outline of Lunna Island barely pierced the mist, while the morning ferry struggled through the towering waves, a lone vessel battling nature's fury.

Moa felt utterly drained. Yet, whenever she reached this breaking point, she had always found a way to claw her way back to life. She would don a mask of happiness, attempting to fool even herself while pouring energy into solving everyone else's problems. But now, once a murmur, the voice inside was screaming. It no longer cared; it was exhausted and didn't know how to carry on.

For as long as Moa could remember, she had believed in the triumph of good and that hard work would always be rewarded. But those comforting beliefs felt distant. The words echoed in her mind, as vivid as ever: Moa, you're the right person in the wrong place. Was it Tomas, her little brother, who had said that? Or maybe her mother? It didn't matter now, as she couldn't ask either.

Moa didn't want to die, yet she couldn't bear to live like this any longer. She wasn't strong enough to pull herself together. Her soul throbbed with sadness and disappointment. Slowly, she filled her lungs with the salty air but didn't dare close her eyes. Another wave crashed against the cliffs, spraying her face with cold droplets, blending with her tears.

She ought to be heading to work; people needed her. Fredrik's missed call still lingered; one she hadn't yet returned. He had promised her beautiful things, and for a moment, she'd allowed herself to believe in them. But, as always, she never learned.

Everything hurt. Every breath, every thought. Life was damned cruel and unfair. A childish thought, perhaps, but she didn't care.

For God's sake, get a grip on yourself, she thought.

Her feet inched closer to the edge. A voice inside her screamed to stop. *You might survive, only to end up in a wheelchair—or worse, trapped in bed with strangers feeding you tasteless food.* The thought taunted her.

A gust of wind shoved her back as her phone rang. Moa staggered before collapsing onto a nearby rock, her breath shaky. Those moments at the cliff's edge felt like a fragment of someone else's life.

"Can you come to work a bit earlier?" Erik Storm, her colleague, snapped her back to reality. "We need to head out immediately. They found a guy sitting in a Ferrari twenty-five meters down. We've got to dive, and I've prepared your dry suit. The coast guard is waiting for us at the port."

Moa stared at the sea, her heart still pounding. *This is important. You are needed and have many reasons to continue living*, her inner voice whispered. And that was enough.

* * *

The rescue boat slowed as it approached the site. Sven Stark, the man who made the emergency call, stood on the deck of an old military vessel. He was no stranger to deep water, training divers for oil and gas platforms in northern Finland and working part-time as a safety officer. However, today, his usual calm was undermined by a flicker of unease in his eyes. Discovering a body twenty-five meters down was far from routine. He had already sent a brief video of the discovery to help facilitate the grim task ahead for the forensic technicians.

"Glad you made it here so quickly," Sven said as he caught the tossed rope. With surprising agility, he leaped onto the rescue boat.

Already in her dry suit, Moa gave her gear a final check. Erik handed her the camera and writing slate, his voice steady yet urgent.

"We hope to retrieve both the body and the car in one dive—there's no time for multiple descents," he explained.

"What were you doing out here near April Islands?" Moa asked, studying Sven, who stood firmly with his legs apart and hands on his hips. His sun-weathered face suggested a man who spent more time outdoors than indoors.

"We were training to navigate with minimal technology," he began. "Given the state of the world, we need to be ready for anything. Today's exercise was supposed to focus on sabotaging gas pipelines. But then the boys surfaced, as white as sheets, claiming they saw a guy sitting in a Ferrari, at the bottom of the sea. Since we started drifting, we reversed and thought we'd practice dead reckoning while there. It seemed like the perfect opportunity."

Sven laughed as if finding a Ferrari underwater was some strange coincidence. "So, I sent down two of our most experienced divers with a camera."

Moa had already sketched a rough layout of the seabed based on the video footage they had sent.

"And the exact coordinates?" Erik asked, slipping on his fins. "We haven't received them yet."

Sven cleared his throat and glanced around. "Yeah, about that, we probably didn't manage to send them. But they're saved on the dive computer. Plus, you have the video."

"We'll log the coordinates ourselves. We're asking you to leave the area," Erik said firmly.

"Yeah, no problem. We'll hang around in case you need any help."

"The area is now classified as a crime scene. You need to leave," Erik insisted, his tone leaving no room for argument.

The rescue divers stood ready with ropes, chains, and a large net. After a quick briefing, everyone was set, and Sven's boat reluctantly drifted away from the site.

"We made some calls and got clearance from Jake Lund, the lawyer," the rescue leader announced. "He's offering one of his heated warehouses at the old port for the car. Would that be useful for you?"

"Perfect," Moa replied. "That way, we can examine it before everything freezes. I'll contact the forensic pathologist once we're nearly ashore so we can meet there."

She slipped extra weights into her vest pockets, glanced at the camera one last time, and fell backward over the railing. Erik followed, vanishing into the icy depths behind her.

CHAPTER TWO

FREDRIK EMPTIED HIS pockets. Keys, access cards, and the phone piled up on his new desk at the police station in Toft. A fresh chapter of his life awaited, but for now, clutter reigned until he found a place for everything.

"Grim Mattis, digital forensic technician." A muscular man, more suited for a sporting goods store, approached with a grin. "My office is at the end of the corridor. Looks like we'll be working together."

"Fredrik Dal, detective inspector specializing in financial crimes. I began my career as a patrol officer, then transitioned to a detective, and have spent the last few years as a forensic technician."

Fredrik shook Grim's hand, noting the firm grip and subtle warmth in his blue eyes.

"Welcome. I heard you had some trouble finding a place to stay?"

"I sorted it out at the last minute." Fredrik offered a brief summary of his life, omitting certain details. "I've been on sick leave since I was shot on duty, but I found a great doctor on the island and lucked into this job. I always wanted to live on an island, and the Friland Islands already feel like home." He hoped this information would stave off further questions. His ex-wife's shopping addiction, the fire that destroyed their house, and the denied insurance claim weren't things Grim needed to know.

"I know who you are," he said with a smirk. "You helped with the Birdman case last year. That was absolutely crazy. Great work."

Fredrik was eager to dive into cold cases and make a difference. "I'm renting a room above The Norse Inn for now, but I plan to look for something more permanent soon."

"That's our second office. Some of us spend more time there than here—breakfast, lunch, meetings, you name it. You're practically living at work already."

Fredrik thought of Moa. He wanted to tell her that the job and housing had come together at the last moment, but reaching out again felt desperate. She hadn't returned his calls, but they would cross paths eventually.

"Maybe I'll stay at the pub. No cooking, no cleaning," Fredrik joked.

Grim let out a laugh. "Just let me know if you need anything. The supplies are in the gray cabinets. The copier's temperamental, but powering it off for five seconds usually does the trick. Oh, and don't forget to place your coffee cup in the dishwasher and leave no crumbs on the table—that's the golden rule. Also, check out The Vault, the staff restaurant on the ground floor. They serve the best lasagna on the island."

"I'm already loving it here," Fredrik replied, pleased with his life choices.

Curiosity drew him to the staff room, where he grabbed a coffee and ran into the prosecutor, Anna Vall. The weight of the past year and the uncertainty of the future began to lift. Friland embraced him once more. He felt confident this was where he would find peace, heal his body and soul, and perhaps even work out again.

He checked his phone, hoping for a message from Moa. Their last conversation had been filled with unresolved emotions. Both tried to clear the air but held back, afraid of vulnerability, and trust was hard-earned. Fredrik resolved to tread carefully, say the right things, and ensure nothing went wrong this time. His badge remained his anchor, even though he was not in uniform this time. He was finally someone.

Sinking into his office chair, Fredrik relaxed, envisioning Moa's smile when she saw him again. His silly daydream was abruptly shattered when Ylva Moore, detective inspector, poked her head through the door.

"Hello, Fredrik, haven't you heard?"

"Heard what?"

"You haven't turned on the radio yet, have you? Moa and Erik received a call. There's a body in a car, twenty-five meters deep. Have you met Grim?"

"I did."

"Good, he's sharp. He'll be working closely with us. We won't have time to slog through paperwork or call logs; his team will handle the grunt work. Welcome to the station. I'll check in later. It's great to see you back on the islands."

Fredrik's phone pinged.

I know where you are.

His heart skipped a beat. It was from an unknown number. He glanced around, almost expecting to see someone watching him, but all he saw was a wintry landscape filled with brick buildings and swaying, leafless trees through the window. Who knew where he was?

He racked his brain but came up empty. No enemies, no grudges. Could Moa have found out he was back?

CHAPTER THREE

AS THE SHADOWY OUTLINE of a car emerged from the depths, Moa's destructive thoughts from the morning at the cliff quickly gave way to the tragedy of reality.

With Erik and two divers beside her, they slowly approached the car, its once glossy red surface now smothered in silt and tangled ocean plants. It seemed to have been resting there for months, ravaged by the sea. Moa snapped photos of the Ferrari from every angle, capturing the eerie stillness as the divers carefully pried open one of the doors.

A thick cloud of silt billowed, engulfing the scene in murkiness. When the water cleared, the grisly truth was revealed—a man strapped into the driver's seat, his face consumed by sea life, his mouth frozen wide in a silent scream.

As usual at a crime scene, Moa felt an intense urge to confront life's injustices and stand with the victims. The man in the car was more than a lifeless body. He was someone's son, perhaps a brother or a husband, taken by a cruel fate. Moa had to detach herself from emotion and concentrate on finding evidence.

While Erik continued taking photos, Moa methodically cut the seatbelt, her movements swift and precise. She spotted a black square bag wedged under the passenger seat. She quickly noted on her slate: *Retrieve the body before investigating further to prevent anything from shifting.*

Erik glanced over and nodded in agreement.

The divers wrapped the body in a net, and Moa watched closely, ensuring it remained intact as they prepared to lift it. The water clouded again as the divers fidgeted unnecessarily. Everyone froze for a few tense minutes, aware that time was against them, especially with safety stops looming during their ascent.

Once the body was removed from the car, Moa focused on the passenger seat. As she shifted to free the bag, she accidentally bumped into the seat, which caused her mask to flood. She tilted her head back, cleared the mask, and mentally reminded herself to stay calm to avoid mistakes. Her fingers grasped the bag, a small, black case capable of holding a camera. She resisted the temptation to open the glove compartment, determined to preserve the scene. Once they had everything safely above the surface, there would be time for that later.

Erik hauled the body wrapped in the net, his movements steady as he waited for Moa while the divers attached chains and cables to the car. With precision, the divers began their ascent, and Moa's gaze swept through the murky water, scanning for anything that might slip from the net. However, all that surrounded them was a swirling cloud of silt and gravel, the eerie stillness making the depths feel even more foreboding.

* * *

Lawyer Jake Lund and forensic pathologist Ida Steen waited at Toft's old port, where summer once brought the hustle and bustle of luxury yachts and excursion boats. Now, the docks lay almost empty, with the only reminder of brighter days being the faded posters plastered on a closed ice cream kiosk, flapping in the cold breeze.

"We found no signs of violence or stab wounds during the initial examination," Moa said, her voice steady. "He was still strapped in the driver's seat. The skin appears waxy, suggesting he has been underwater for quite a while."

Ida agreed. "You are right. All I can do now is prepare an official report and take dental impressions. Estimating the time of death at a few months, at least."

Her tone was flat as she recorded her findings in a monotonous manner. The dank smell of death spiraled through the air, settling like a thick, unwelcome presence.

"Are you two done here?" she asked, not waiting for a response. "I'll call Falck to pick up the body."

"Perfect. We'll move on to the car," Moa said, heading toward the warehouse.

Erik ended a call and turned to Moa. "Ylva checked the registration. The car belongs to Benny Palm, who has been missing since April third."

"That's right, it's Benny, the photographer. Nobody could have missed him driving around in a Ferrari," Moa recalled.

Jake stepped into the room as the car was being wheeled in. "Are you sure it's him?" he asked. "Benny was my client."

"We're waiting for a formal identification," Moa replied, "but all signs point to him."

Jake's expression darkened. "That's unfortunate. Hopefully, you'll discover something in the car. I'll arrange for a couple of security guards to monitor things tonight."

"That won't be necessary," Erik replied firmly. "We'll have a patrol stationed here until the forensic investigation is complete."

Moa meticulously labeled the evidence bag containing the camera bag. She would examine it back at the station, away from prying eyes.

"Tell the patrol not to let anyone else in," she whispered to Erik.

"I've already made sure of that," he replied. "Funny how many people suddenly want to 'help,' yet no one seems to have seen or heard anything when a patrol knocks on the door asking for witnesses."

Moa rubbed her hands vigorously before the car's heater vent, trying to warm her frozen fingers.

"Ylva called," Erik said. "She wants a quick meeting when we get back to the station. She's eager to get started. We'll change, grab a bite, and then check the car this afternoon."

"Sounds good. I'm freezing," Moa replied, her breath fogging the window. "By the way, do you know why a lawyer has a warehouse down by the port?"

"Jake runs several businesses, but the largest is recycling tires. They grind them down and use the material for construction projects. He ships a lot of it overseas; somewhere in Africa, I think."

"Right, I've heard about that. Oh, look." She pointed as they passed the town hall. "Graffiti again. What a shame. Those numbers are appearing all over town. Is it a band or something?"

Erik shrugged. "I wouldn't know. I can't keep up with every new trend."

Moa checked her phone and noticed a brief message from Kajsa asking her to call when she had a moment. She stared at it for a second, feeling a knot of tension tightening in her chest. She thought she had everything under control, but now she felt a creeping unease, an unsettling awareness that something was about to change very soon.

CHAPTER FOUR

MOA HANDED THE camera to the digital forensics team without hesitation. Time was ticking, and she had no reason to handle the camera or film rolls.

She locked herself in the restroom, her fingers moving to tug off the wig that had become a daily burden. Despite the hairnet, the strands were tangled, and she was tired of pretending. Her hair had attempted to grow back in patches, but she had lost the energy to care due to the weight of recent stress. Perhaps it was time to face the world without the wig—embrace the curious stares and get used to explaining alopecia.

She picked up her phone and called Kajsa, who answered immediately.

"What's happened?" Moa asked.

"Your mom is having trouble breathing. The ventilator is acting up, but someone from the medical supplies center is bringing a replacement. Don't worry, I can stay tonight if you need me to," she reassured her.

Moa fought back tears. Kajsa was her rock, the one person she could lean on when the world was crumbling down.

"You need sleep," Kajsa stated. "She'll understand. I'll set up the air mattress and stay with her tonight."

"Will Susanne be able to come tomorrow?" Moa asked, desperate for a solution.

"No, her whole family caught a stomach bug. But don't worry, we'll figure it out. I'll stay as long as necessary. That's what we agreed on."

Moa closed her eyes, a wave of gratitude washing over her, even as the uncertainty of the future pressed tighter around her.

She would have sent Fredrik a message if there had been a moment to spare. He had called multiple times, always at the worst times, and there was no time for idle conversation. She had long stopped waiting for him to return to the islands.

* * *

Ylva Moore was already in the meeting room, flipping through a stack of papers. Her crisp gray suit starkly contrasted with the casual look of Moa and Erik's uniforms. Outside, the icy morning wind had softened into a gentle breeze, now carrying rain.

"Where's Grim?" Ylva asked, glancing up. "I told him to be here. Has anyone seen him?"

"Let's give him a few minutes," Erik said. "The elevator is out, and it's a long hike up three flights."

"And Fredrik Dal," Ylva continued, "whom some of you know, starts today. His paperwork was finalized more quickly than expected, and he'll join us shortly."

Moa felt a pang of guilt for not returning Fredrik's calls. He had promised to return, but she never imagined he'd become her colleague. The last time they spoke, he was starting a course in Stockholm, and she figured he'd settled in mainland Sweden for good. But when Fredrik arrived with Grim, it felt like no time had passed. He caught her eye and smiled before settling beside Ylva, who immediately began the meeting.

"I've reviewed Benny Palm's missing person report and will continue to work on it until we get an official identification," Ylva said. "I expect to receive dental records from Ida later today, so we should have confirmation by this afternoon."

Moa's mind raced, barely focusing on the report. Seeing Fredrik again stirred up more than old memories—it felt like a storm she hadn't prepared for. "We're attending the autopsy tomorrow," she said.

Ylva leaned forward. "What's your first impression?"

Moa took a sip of water before responding. "Dumping a Ferrari at the bottom of the sea isn't something you do on a whim. It requires resources; this wasn't a quick job. A winch was probably involved. We'll inspect the chassis this afternoon for signs of any damage. Since the car wasn't intended to be recovered, no precautions were likely taken to protect it during the winching process. All the windows were slightly open, allowing the car to flood and sink in seconds. There's no evidence of violence, so we assume he was already dead when the car went down."

Erik remained quiet, letting Moa take the lead as she often did, even though he was the forensic coordinator.

"Grim, any updates?" Ylva asked, shifting her attention.

"Yes, I'm working closely with the image analysis team on the camera Moa recovered. We started right away. An analog film roll was inside the bag, and the canister was sealed tightly. Hopefully, the film is still usable—older gear like this can be quite reliable."

"Good. I expect to get more information about the car later," Ylva said, her gaze shifting to Moa and Erik. "Can I expect the preliminary report before the end of the day?"

Moa realized it would be well past six before they wrapped up. "We'll get the report together, but it will take the time needed."

"As you've probably noticed, Fredrik is back on the islands," Ylva added, casually including him in the conversation. "Last time he was here, things got pretty dramatic in Nordby. This time, he'll be working closely with Grim and me. Depending on how the case evolves, we might need to bring in more people."

Ylva wrapped up the meeting.

CHAPTER FIVE

IT FELT ALMOST SURREAL to Fredrik, as if the universe were playing some trick on him. Not long ago, he had found himself with the same group of officers, entangled in a high-profile murder case. Back then, he was a wreck—broke, lost, and nursing constant pain from his injured shoulder. But now, everything was different. Hanna, the sharp, no-nonsense assistant from the hotel he had stayed at last year, had taken over the local pub—The Norse Inn—in Toft.

"It's great to see everyone back together!" She laughed, placing down the menus. "Today's special is our take on the classic Scandinavian smorgasbord."

Grim and Erik started piling food onto their plates while Moa anxiously switched off her phone. Her eyes darted around the room, as if searching for the right words.

"I won't ask why you didn't tell me you were back," she told Fredrik. "I'm sorry for not returning your calls. No excuses. It's just that things have been a bit crazy lately."

"How have you been? Did you not believe me when I said I'd be back for good?" Fredrik asked with a smile.

Moa hesitated for a moment, then replied, "Yes and no. I believed you'd return, but I never imagined we'd be working together on the same case. Congratulations, though, and welcome to Friland. It's good to see you again."

Her words were warm, but her eyes revealed a flicker of resignation.

"Thanks. I'm renting a room upstairs for now," he said. "You should stop by with a pizza one evening."

They shared a laugh as their memories bubbled up while they made their way to the buffet.

"Is that Ingrid behind the counter?" Moa asked.

Ingrid's sullen expression and long blonde hair, like a doll come to life, were unmistakable. She poured a frothy beer for a tall man with tangled hair.

"It's her."

Moa shook her head in disbelief. "I know she wasn't involved in the murders or that she knew her husband was a serial killer, but she's the last person I expected to see here."

Fredrik said, "Let's grab some food. We have a lot to catch up on."

The Norse Inn, nestled in the heart of Toft, exuded medieval charm. Wooden walls, sturdy tables, and wrought-iron fixtures provided a rustic vibe. An open fire crackled in the hearth, spreading a cozy warmth throughout the room, while the soft, dim lighting offered a welcome break from the sterile brightness of the office. Fredrik's small upstairs room continued with the same rustic theme, compact and simple, yet he grew to appreciate its cozy minimalism. It stood in stark contrast to the seven-room villa outside Stockholm, but surprisingly, it suited him.

"There's been talk of bringing on new staff for a while now," Erik said as he joined them, "but I never expected you'd be one of us."

Fredrik smiled, a warm glow spreading through him. It felt good to be back.

One of us.

Those three little words meant so much to him. Finally, he felt like he belonged to something bigger, no longer feeling useless at home. He was part of a team, contributing something meaningful to society.

"I realized I couldn't return to forensic work after my injury," Fredrik said, "so I transitioned to detective inspector and specialized in financial crimes."

"Good move," Grim replied. "We've seen a surge of opportunists lately, starting businesses in the gray zone—mostly young Swedes from the mainland hoping to turn Friland into the next Malta due to its favorable tax laws. Thankfully, we've shut down any talk of casinos. We want to keep the islands peaceful for as long as possible."

"But people are always inventive when it comes to making quick money," Moa said.

Their eyes drifted to a man at the bar with a rough-looking homemade tattoo on his hand. The air shifted as tension built. A scuffle erupted, and he began shouting and slurring curses. Grim shot to his feet, his towering frame moving swiftly. The drunk, tangled-haired man with the tattoo was quickly escorted out, still swearing under his breath. Hanna shook her head, offering Grim a grateful smile.

His muscular build was usually enough to keep trouble at bay, and most assumed he was a lifeguard, given his imposing presence.

"He seems to be carrying a lot on his shoulders. That and a few too many beers are rarely a good combination," Grim said as he sat down.

"Isn't it a bit early in the day to start trouble? Did he say anything?" Moa asked.

"He mostly rambled and repeated that we don't understand anything, that it's all terrible, and that the world is ending soon."

Everyone laughed and ordered coffee.

"We're heading to the old port to continue examining the car," Erik said, looking at Fredrik.

"I'll check up on Benny Palm and await Ylva's instructions," Fredrik replied.

"You can find a lot of useful information if you search for Benny's name," Erik said. "He got caught up in a bit of trouble last year. His artist sister stole several of his photos, mostly from a series, and used them in her works. It was obvious they were copied. Benny often exhibited his photos and had several for sale in limited editions. He sued her for copyright infringement. Wasn't the lawyer we met this morning handling the case?"

Erik turned to Moa, who said, "Yes, Jake Lund. They won the case against the sister. If you're already well-known and have clientele, why would you need to steal someone else's work?"

Fredrik thanked Ingrid as she brought their coffee. He couldn't help but wonder how she was coping with the grief after her husband's death and adjusting to being an employee instead of bossing Hanna around. Ingrid's life had taken a sharp turn.

"It's the new normal, with everyone copying everything because they want stuff for free. Nobody's willing to put in the effort anymore," Grim said, shaking his head. "And trust me, it will get worse before it gets better. If people used half the energy they spent cheating and taking shortcuts on something legal and productive, the world would look different. But then again"—he smirked—"we'd all be out of jobs. So, I rest my case."

He chuckled at his joke, glancing down as his phone buzzed.

"It was the image analysis team; they have developed the film and found pictures."

CHAPTER SIX

CAPITANOS KNEW PLENTY who craved a slice of the pie, convinced they were entitled to it. They couldn't see they were pawns in a game they'd never win. The idea that anyone could succeed, no matter what, was pure nonsense. Success required grit and action, not wishful thinking. At some point, you had to draw the line.

"Tonight, as usual. Are you ready?"

The man hesitated, but he knew he was in too deep to say no. He needed the money.

"Yes, everything's set."

Maybe it was time to teach him what happened when resources ran dry and make him understand the gravity of his role. Capitanos entertained the thought of stripping him of his comfort, forcing him into desperation. A little variety never hurts. Violence was satisfying, but there was something disturbingly fulfilling in breaking a man down and watching him struggle to survive.

"The seas will be rough. Do you understand the risks?" the man asked, a hint of nerves creeping into his voice.

"I love risks," Capitanos replied smoothly. "Tonight, then."

A door slammed shut, and the air thickened with a scent that suggested luxury and danger, a lingering trace of life's finest excesses. It enveloped the man left alone in the basement, haunted by his dependence on a master he didn't dare defy.

Tonight, then. He had no other choice.

CHAPTER SEVEN

THE AIR INSIDE the warehouse was thick with the damp smell of wet car seats, and puddles of saltwater had already formed on the floor. The patrol on duty mentioned that it had been quiet, no nosy onlookers and no press.

"I'd like to bring the seats back to the lab," Erik said, glancing at the soaked interior. "But leaving them overnight is not ideal. Let's examine them here, see what we find, and if needed, we can move them tomorrow."

Their voices echoed through the warehouse, and despite the faint warmth inside, the dampness seeped into their clothes. Moa shivered, briefly envying Fredrik, no crawling around on cold stone floors for evidence. She longed for a desk job, even entertaining the thought of returning to crime investigation.

"Do you think there's good money in tire recycling?" she mused aloud.

Erik chuckled, seeming to catch her drift. "Considering a career change?"

"Yes, especially on days like these," she said, smiling. "But then, when it all comes together, it's worth the cold, the damp, and the occasional misery."

They divided the tasks, with Erik taking photos and Moa noting them. They started to work, systematically scanning the floor for anything that might have washed out of the car.

Ylva's message chimed, and Moa gave Erik a thumbs-up.

"Ida worked quickly," she said. "The dental records confirm it's the photographer, Benny Palm."

"Well, that gives us a place to start," Erik stated.

"For now, dental records are reliable. They're impossible to fake, and thankfully, we haven't had any cases with ground-down teeth," Moa added dryly, pocketing her phone before shifting her focus to the car's chassis. She examined it section by section, noting that it was almost untouched, with no scratches or signs of impact.

Erik said, "These tires appear brand new. That makes sense for a luxury car like this. The Coast Guard and marine police will have their hands full with this case."

"Most likely, they chose a heavily trafficked route. It's like looking for a needle in a haystack," Moa said as she moved to inspect the driver's seat. The chances of finding preserved evidence were slim. Their evidence bags rarely looked that empty.

"Nothing but sand from the seabed," Moa muttered, opening the glove compartment.

Inside, the water had fused everything—a leather-bound notebook reduced to pulp stuck to a water bottle, sunglasses, and a tangle of cables.

"A shame about the notebook," Moa murmured. "But maybe there's more to find at his house. Will we have time for that tomorrow?"

"We should be able to, as long as we don't have to return here."

"No phone, no personal belongings, his pockets were empty. We'll need to pull out the seats to inspect every inch. This is going to take time," Moa sighed. "I'll call the dealership to find out what tools we need."

Setting aside his notepad, Erik said, "Let's do that, and I'll arrange to bring the car closer to the station. I don't want it left here overnight."

Moa knelt on the damp floor, reluctantly shining her flashlight under the driver's seat. With long tweezers, she fished out a small, rough white stone about three centimeters in diameter.

"Finally, something. Looks like limestone."

The thrill of the discovery briefly made her forget the ache from crouching for nearly three hours. Mentally, she experienced a boost, a reminder that every small find mattered.

"Nice work," Erik said, reaching for a bag and carefully labeling it with the date and location. "There's only one limestone quarry on the islands, on Breda. The stone could come from a garden. This one looks polished."

"Or from the bottom? Or a random stone? From anywhere on the islands?"

CHAPTER EIGHT

THE PALE AFTERNOON sun made a feeble attempt to pierce the window of Fredrik's office, casting a dim glow over his cluttered desk. The corridor was silent—one of the things he appreciated most about the job. Outsiders liked to call it the "efficient Nordic silence." Despite the team's intense focus on solving brutal crimes, the work was conducted calmly and professionally, without unnecessary noise or drama. Tasks were managed with precision and quietly. Occasionally, the police radio crackled with an alert—a reminder of the world beyond—but it required no immediate attention.

"I've sent you the photos," Grim said, clearing some books from a chair and pulling it closer to the desk before sitting down.

"Great, let's have a look."

Fredrik straightened his back, realizing he had been slouching. His left shoulder began to ache after lunch, but he reassured himself that his upcoming appointment with Dr. Ulrik would help. He hoped that the humidity on Friland would be gentler on his joints than the winters on the mainland.

"You can always count on good old analog film," Grim noted. "Let me know if you want any of them printed."

Fredrik opened the folder, discovering twenty-four black-and-white images. More than half were minimalistic scenes, the kind Benny was known for, images that, while barely detailed, conveyed a calming simplicity.

"These last seven shots," Grim said, pointing to photos of various boats, "might be the ones worth looking into."

"Yeah, it almost looks like he was out on a shoot and stumbled upon something unexpected. Or maybe he was actively searching for new material? These aren't your average leisure boats."

"Exactly. These are high-end yachts worth millions. And if you zoom in on the second-to-last photo, you can spot a small port. It looks like the lighthouse on Breda Island in the background. I'm waiting for more photos from someone over there—saves me the trip."

"Take a look at this. Someone is standing on one of the boats. He might be significant?"

Grim leaned in as Fredrik focused on the image. A middle-aged man with sharp features and pointed ears stood distinctly on deck.

"Maybe. I'll see if I can enhance it without compromising clarity."

As Fredrik examined the pictures, he felt the old urge to take up photography again, his mind brimming with ideas. He was sure that moving to the Friland Islands had been the right choice, and he felt his creativity flowing.

"Oh, and by the way," Fredrik added, "Ylva called. They confirmed the body belongs to Benny Palm. Anna suggested we speak to his sister. I'll look into his finances, request call logs, and arrange a meeting with the lawyer involved."

He flipped open his notepad. "Jake Lund at JL Law. That case involving the sister who stole Benny's images might hold some clues."

Fredrik's phone buzzed with a new message, pulling his attention back.

Do you like pizza?

The message came from an unknown number, but Fredrik was sure it was Moa up to something unusual—even if games weren't her style. He almost replied but switched off the phone.

"I'll follow up on the photos," Grim said. "By the way, the guy stirring up trouble at The Norse Inn yesterday is a sailor, and a regular who seems to know everyone around. It might be worth checking in with him if you see him there. He's an odd character, and I'm unsure which side of the law he's on."

"Good to know, my list keeps getting longer," Fredrik replied, scanning his notes. "It turns out the caller, Sven

Stark, also works as the security officer for FONG on the oil platform near Torshamn. Have there been any recent incidents?"

Starting fresh on the job was always challenging, but being new to the islands made it even trickier. Fredrik was casting a wide net, unafraid to dig deeper. Sometimes, you struck gold; other times, you found nothing.

"FONG's reputable," Grim replied. "A few minor incidents—some employees in drunken brawls, but nothing serious."

"And Sven? I assume he has a clean record to hold that position?"

"Or maybe the opposite—a job like that could be the perfect cover."

"We have hundreds of sailors to consider questioning, along with customs staff, dockworkers, and warehouse security."

"Right, and the new port in Toft operates differently than the old one. The warehouses at the old port are more of a gray area." Grim chuckled, giving Fredrik a pat on the back. "Good luck with that list," he said before heading out.

Fredrik called Sven Stark, who answered immediately, reiterating the limited information already covered in Erik and Moa's report. Sven mentioned he would be working double shifts for the next few days and wouldn't have time to meet for at least two days.

Fredrik checked Sven's criminal record for any leads but found nothing. Nonetheless, his instincts suggested that the biggest fish often swam in the smallest ponds.

CHAPTER NINE

MOA RELUCTANTLY PLACED her private gun into the safe hidden in a kitchen cabinet. Sometimes, she needed to feel the cold, sleek metal of her Walther, running her fingers along the barrel and resting them on the trigger. The Walther was more than just a weapon; it was a symbol of strength that kept her going. After spending her childhood throwing darts in the basement, she received her first air pistol on her tenth birthday—a gift from a neighbor who was a member of the local shooting club. From that moment on, she felt she had found her true calling. Shooting ranges, competitions, and trophies quickly replaced her nights out during her teenage years. She continued with shooting, a decision she was grateful for when she applied to join the police force.

Her mom, Vera, had worsened throughout the day, but as soon as she saw her daughter step through the door, a sense of relief softened her face, bringing a fragile calm.

"I'm here," Moa murmured, gently touching her mother's arm. "It is what it is, as you always used to say."

An iPad was propped up on the bookshelf, displaying a live feed of her brother Tomas in his apartment. Moa's gaze lingered on him, a wave of sickness and dread filling the room.

"I'm here. All night," she repeated softly, reassuring them both.

"Yeah." Vera's voice was barely a whisper but steady. Moa tried not to dwell on the things her mother wished she could say but couldn't. Vera had always shared gossip and recipes with neighbors, gave talks at the library, and was a cheerful soul who never let the silence settle for long.

"I'm going to freshen up, and then we'll make something to eat with Kajsa."

For now, everyday life was on pause. When her mother was gone, Moa knew her focus would shift entirely to Tomas, ensuring he received the best rehabilitation and care.

Vera lowered her gaze. Her hair was greasy and needed washing, and her biggest fear was becoming a smelly burden. Her left arm lay immobilized in a splint, and each day her strength slipped further away.

Tomas's life had taken a tragic turn during what was supposed to be a joyful return. While en route from the airport, his taxi collided with a tanker. The driver was drunk and walked away unscathed. A witness managed to pull Tomas from the wreckage in time, though he was left with life-changing injuries. After seven years on the Faroe Islands, Tomas was excited to make a fresh start back home, surprising his sister with a job and a new place to live. Instead, he now sat in a wheelchair at a state rehabilitation center, his dreams put on hold.

"It'll be cold tonight. Did you have a busy day?" Kajsa asked, buttoning her cardigan.

"A bit," Moa replied. "We pulled a body from twenty-five meters down—a strange scene. Even with dry suits, it was freezing. Days like this make me long for a regular desk job."

"You're doin' great," Vera whispered, dabbing at her dark blue sweatpants with a tissue as if wiping away an invisible stain.

Tomas was paralyzed from the waist down, and his body was covered in scars from burns; his hearing was nearly gone. It had been only months since the accident, and the doctors warned that his recovery would be long, possibly years. Moa had vowed to ensure he received the best care, no matter the cost. But reality was harsh, and resources were limited.

They had dreams yet to be fulfilled. They had discussed traveling to the Greek islands, skydiving, and swimming with dolphins. Moa was determined: Tomas would not be left to languish in a worn-down state facility. Not while there was still so much for them to accomplish.

The first sign was a tingling sensation in her mom's left hand the day after Tomas's accident. The doctors dismissed it as being due to stress and grief, but the symptoms escalated rapidly. Within months, she received a diagnosis of ALS. Living alone became a challenge, and Moa vowed to ensure her mother's remaining time, however brief, was dignified.

"Tomas is doing well," she said, her voice sounding hollow as she gestured toward him on the screen. She had to believe it was true.

Tomas sat by the window in his room while an assistant helped him eat. His arms were still healing, each movement clearly painful, and he wore a cap while waiting for his hair to regrow after the last surgery. Moa turned on the sound, hoping to shatter the heavy silence.

"Hi, Tomas."

The assistant turned—a familiar face Moa had nicknamed the Sweaty and Miserable. She nudged Tomas's shoulder, and he slowly turned to the screen. Moa leaned into Vera and raised her hand to greet him.

* * *

Later, they shared a meal and casually chatted about home decor. The conversation drifted to Moa's sparsely decorated townhouse. Experts might describe it as "Scandinavian minimalism"—featuring earthy tones and minimal clutter. Vera thought it could benefit from some warmth: candle holders, pillows, and paintings. However, Moa had always preferred to fill her space with happy memories rather than material items. She pretended to be interested, and Kajsa played along.

"You know," Kajsa said with a wink, "a couple of small tables with some green plants by the window would fit perfectly."

"Mirrors," Vera murmured, a spark of interest flickering in her eyes. Moa forced herself to play along and be polite.

"Maybe in that corner. Sure, why not?" she replied, slipping into the role, even as her skin prickled at the thought.

The new ventilator seemed to be helping; Vera's breathing was steadier, and she looked a bit stronger. In the hallway, Kajsa leaned in close.

"Have you decided about the house?" she whispered.

Lacing up her boots, Moa said, "I'm sticking to the plan we discussed. See if the guys you mentioned can handle everything—container and sorting, preferably within a few days. I can't manage it with a full-time job, and I lack the time or energy. I want it cleared out."

"Photos? Memories?"

"The last time I opened a box, it was filled with CDs. They might have been photos—most weren't labeled, with random dates scattered throughout. And that was just one box in a five-room house. I have all the memories I need right here," she said, tapping her temple. "And honestly, that's more than enough."

"I understand. I'll reach out to them."

"Thank you. The sooner it's done, the better."

"Okay. If you need a break this week, I'll bring Vera back to the house for a while. I think she'd like that."

Moa's eyes filled with tears as she stepped outside. She replied to Fredrik's message, saying she'd like to meet the next day. Reluctantly, she dialed her dad's number, silently hoping it would go to voicemail.

CHAPTER TEN

THE WIND HOWLED as rain pounded against the windows of The Norse Inn. Fredrik reflected on his first day at work, realizing he had not had enough time to explore all the details he wished to investigate. Hanna arrived with a sandwich and a steaming pot of tea.

"As of today, you have a new neighbor," she stated, setting the tray down. "Ingrid. She'll be in the room next to yours until she's back on her feet."

Fredrik blinked, surprised. He wasn't sure he had the energy to deal with a strange neighbor. She didn't say much, but you could never know what to expect from her.

"Understood," he replied, eyeing the neatly stacked layers on his sandwich: thick slices of cheese, ham with a hint of mustard, cucumber, and vibrant red tomatoes on dark rye.

As he took a bite, he noticed Ingrid scrolling through her phone, occasionally glancing at the empty bar. In the corner sat the same man Grim had escorted out the previous night. Fredrik decided to approach him later; as a regular, he would likely linger until closing time.

Fredrik shifted back to the food, savoring each bite, when Hanna cleared a nearby table, leaning in as if she could read his thoughts. "He's not drunk today, just angry," she remarked, gesturing toward the man with a wry smile.

"Every place has its character," Fredrik stated as he took another bite.

"Tore Viklund, sailor and regular," Hanna said. "It took him ages to accept me as the new owner. He pays his tab like clockwork but never leaves a cent as a tip."

Near the fireplace, a woman sat with a young girl across from her. The woman wore a leopard-print jacket over tight white leggings, paired with bright pink high heels, looking completely engrossed in her phone. Her lips, plumped with fillers, curled into a smile as she tapped and swiped at the screen, while her untouched salad wilted beside her. The child, no older than five, tapped her chubby fingers on a greasy tablet screen, focused on a matching game, casting hopeful glances at the woman for attention. Occasionally, the woman offered a distracted word of praise without looking up, and when she wasn't watching, the girl stuck out her tongue in defiance.

Fredrik browsed his phone, seeking information on Benny Palm. The search yielded pages about the notorious copyright infringement case involving his stolen photos, along with recent headlines announcing his death. The police were urging anyone with information to come forward.

Switching between Benny's website, where his online shop was hosted, and the latest news, Fredrik studied the photographer's style. Benny's images, framed in a square like those shot on a Hasselblad, were predominantly in black and white or soft grayscale, evoking a minimalist calm.

Fredrik felt inspired and decided to head out with his camera and backpack, ready for an impromptu shoot.

A deep foghorn cut through the pub's low hum, echoing between the buildings and accompanied by a dog's bark. He had heard the sound before and asked Hanna about it as she passed his table.

"The old foghorn sounds every weekday at nine, signaling that the day has ended. It serves as a reminder to lock up and rest," Hanna said. "It has been a tradition here since medieval times, and most folks are so accustomed to it that they don't even hear it anymore."

"It's a good idea to have something old and familiar," Fredrik replied, "especially with so much chaos in the world right now."

Hanna smiled as she greeted a man heading toward Tore's table.

Fredrik's thoughts shifted to Benny, who, according to Google, lived in a comfortable apartment in Toft, nestled in a quiet neighborhood where the residents appeared well-off. Next on his list was to visit the apartment as soon as the forensic technicians completed their investigation. He relied on them to uncover something that could lead to Benny's killer.

The woman in the leopard-print jacket finally set down her phone and picked at her salad. Her young daughter, kicking her legs on the chair, scooped up chocolate ice cream, letting it drip down her chin onto the tablet screen. She sucked on a sticky finger and then swiped it across the tablet, leaving chocolate streaks mixed with saliva on the glossy surface.

The man who joined Tore resembled the figure he had seen in Benny's photos. Even from a distance, the man's pointed ears were unmistakable. Maybe it was wishful thinking, his mind eager to find a lead after a long day. He knew he needed rest—exhaustion wouldn't help him make a good impression on his new team. Mistakes weren't an option right now.

After settling his tab, Fredrik asked Hanna, who seemed to know everyone, if she had ever seen the man with the pointed ears. She hadn't. With that, he headed up to his room and called Moa, having looked forward to hearing her voice.

"Of course, I like pizza," Fredrik chuckled.

"Good, because you're the one who suggested it," Moa teased.

"By the way, I noticed you used an unknown number when you texted me—any reason for that?"

As he unlocked his door and stepped inside, he heard the hum of traffic outside and felt a surprising sense of comfort. In his small room, he almost felt at home.

"I didn't, and I don't know what you're talking about. Look, I just got back from the gym and need a shower. Can we plan to meet soon? I have a few things to sort out first, but let's catch up after the meeting tomorrow afternoon. And yes, I'd love to share a pizza."

Fredrik was about to close his phone when another message flashed on the screen:

First day on the job. Just arrived on the island. You don't want to lose this job, do you?

The tone had shifted, sending a chill up Fredrik's spine. This was more than a prank.

CHAPTER ELEVEN

THE TEAM HAD GATHERED at the Toft station for a morning meeting. A faint scent of coffee lingered in the air.

"Have you heard about Ylva?" Fredrik asked, placing his coffee on the table. He continued without waiting for a response, "She had an accident involving a boat. She was driving behind a trailer when the boat came loose and fell off, hitting her car."

"Good grief," Moa said.

She always experienced goosebumps and a wave of nausea when she heard about traffic accidents, especially when they involved people she knew.

"Is she hurt?"

"She called from the hospital," Fredrik said. "They're keeping her for a few days for observation. She is in a great deal of pain, has a concussion, and both of her wrists are broken. Her husband is with her. She is very shaken up. A few more centimeters, and she would have been crushed." He paused, then added, "I've been ordered to lead the investigation into Benny's murder and bring in any extra personnel I might need."

Grim said, "I heard the call come in over the radio," he continued. "It almost sounded comical—a car colliding with a boat. But now that we know the facts, it's anything but funny."

"Let's get started," Erik said. "Moa and I attended Benny's autopsy this morning. Ida confirmed that the cause of death was due to drowning. He was alive when the car sank; perhaps he was unconscious, and there were no indications of injury. We'll wait to see what the lab reports reveal about any substances found in his blood."

"You mentioned the windows were open?" Grim asked, making a note.

"Partially," Erik confirmed.

"Enough to flood the car quickly," Moa added. "So far, all we have are the photos from his camera—and this." She held up a small evidence bag containing a polished white stone.

"A limestone," she continued. "It looks like the kind used in garden decor. While it could be a coincidence that it ended up in his car, there's not a scratch on the vehicle, so we suspect it might've been tipped off a ramp from a larger vessel. After the meeting, we'll search Benny's apartment to see if we spot anything similar."

"Or any links to limestones," Erik noted. "Breda Island has a large limestone quarry, so it's common to see these stones in people's gardens around here."

Fredrik, sitting quietly, stood up and pointed at the noticeboard Ylva had set up for the case. At the center, a note with "Benny Palm?" was pinned in the middle.

"We can replace this," he said, attaching a photo of Benny at the top. "The shots from Benny's camera show seven photos of the port in Breda with luxury boats, and a man with pointed ears is in the background. I don't know if he's connected to the boats, but I could swear I saw him talking to Tore Vikholm—the drunken sailor at The Norse Inn—last night. Hanna gave me some background on Tore, so I'll question him as soon as possible."

Fredrik pinned one of the port photos next to Benny's and continued, "Benny was reported missing by his sister, Claire. The patrolman who informed her of his death said she took it calmly, almost as if she weren't surprised. We need to locate a laptop or phone at Benny's place. Grim, what do you have?"

"I skimmed Benny's social media history. He was active in a few photography groups about two years ago, mostly discussing copyright issues. Someone called Klara made harsh, antagonistic comments and clashed with him in several threads. I think it might have been his sister, Claire. I've pulled out the key exchanges in a report. They seemed to dislike each other."

Fredrik glanced around, processing the information.

"We're heading to Benny's apartment," Erik said. "Let's stay in touch and update each other throughout the day."

Moa brushed pastry crumbs off the table and gathered her belongings. She had so much to share with Fredrik but felt the words slipping away. A lot had changed since they last spoke.

"Do you think you'll have time to meet tonight?" Fredrik asked.

"Sure, I'd love to. Pizza at your humble abode?"

"Nope. We're eating out—it's my treat. There's a little place near the square, The Loft. I've heard great things about it. Do you know it?"

"Oh, it looks so cozy! I've wanted to go there for ages but never found the time."

As Moa headed to her car, a spark of hope ignited a warmth she hadn't experienced in a long time.

CHAPTER TWELVE

A STALE, MUSTY ODOR clung to the air as Moa and Erik entered Benny's apartment. The clock on the kitchen wall had stopped at a quarter to eleven, and a brown towel lay on the floor in front of the open fridge.

"Lucky someone emptied and turned off the fridge," Erik muttered, wrinkling his nose. "I'll open a few windows, so we don't get headaches."

The blinds were down, and the power was off. Moa placed her forensic bag in the center of the room and surveyed the scene, trying to piece together clues about Benny's daily life. Who was he? What drove him? Did he sit at his desk every night to edit photos and eat in front of the TV? Where would he keep the things that mattered most?

The apartment was a jumble of spaces, a bedroom strewn with clothes and belongings, a living room that doubled as an office and TV area. The bathroom had been transformed into a darkroom, stacked high with black-and-white photos. The kitchen was almost eerily clean, except for the towel on the floor.

"Looks like he didn't cook much," Moa observed.

Erik scanned his flashlight over the empty kitchen counters. Two coffee mugs rested in the sink.

"Seems right. A couple of pizza boxes are tucked under the sofa," he said. "I'll grab a few lights from the van."

Moa forced herself to concentrate on the job, trying to block out thoughts of her mother, her brother, and now Fredrik—a flicker of hope she wasn't willing to lose. It had been an overwhelming stretch lately, and she wasn't sure how much to share with Fredrik.

As Erik set up the lights, her phone buzzed with a message from her lifesaver and private investigator, Vilda.

I need help. You owe me one. Call as soon as you have time.

"Everything okay?" Erik asked.

"All good. Let's start at the desk. Benny likely spent most of his time here, and I wouldn't be surprised if he ate his dinner while he worked."

Moa opened a few cabinets at random, her mind drifting to Vilda. A favor was owed, but the timing couldn't be worse. Moa could only hope Vilda needed money—that would be easier than risking bending any rules. In the last cabinet, Moa found rows of cameras neatly lined up. Shining her flashlight inside, she called Erik.

"This must have been his passion. Was he a collector? But this seems a bit excessive. How much is all this worth?" she wondered aloud, jotting down notes.

"You'd need a solid income to afford all that gear. Take a closer look at the desk and the drawers," Erik instructed, his tone pulling her back into focus. "We need to start somewhere."

Moa methodically searched the desk drawers, picking out a few notebooks. Erik uncovered two laptops and a desktop computer.

"I'll search the bathroom," Moa said, sifting through piles of black-and-white photos. Each photo featured warehouses with nearly identical doors.

"Was he obsessed with the patterns on the warehouse doors?" she asked, holding up a few shots for Erik to see.

Erik shook his head in frustration. "Fredrik's not going to be thrilled. There are countless warehouses on these islands, and they all look alike. Do you see any patterns here? Are there any negatives?" Without waiting, he continued, "Let's bring everything to Grim and the image analysis team. Grim's sharp; he might notice something."

Moa began packing the photos and negatives, carefully labeling each bag.

There were no dental appointment notes, shopping lists, or anything on the fridge—not even a single magnet. It was likely that such items would stay digital, complicating some aspects of her job and increasing demands within the department. A hastily written note could signify an early breakthrough in an investigation.

She bagged the coffee cups separately, labeling them by date and location. Perhaps Benny had shared coffee with someone on the day he disappeared.

Moa paused at one of the framed photographs, a striking black-and-white image of foamy waves crashing against jagged rocks. On impulse, she lifted the frame and looked behind it. The photo's title read: "The Ocean Provides, and the Ocean Reclaims."

Frustrated by the lack of evidence, she glanced at the desk again, feeling time slip away.

"Where have I seen these numbers before?" Erik muttered, examining a manual with a fifteen-digit number written in the margin.

"Maybe it's a password or a phone number with a country code?" she suggested. "Let's bag it and investigate."

Moa was sure she'd seen that number somewhere before—but where?

CHAPTER THIRTEEN

FREDRIK HAD RECEIVED photos of Benny's modest apartment, which starkly contrasted with his sister's villa.

An expansive glass veranda stretched from the front entrance to the backyard, while the garden was lined with small conifers bordering winding paths of white gravel.

Claire greeted him with a firm handshake and a steady gaze.

"We weren't close," she said, offering coffee, which Fredrik politely declined.

The pristine white walls of the living room were adorned with vibrant artwork, and a drowsy Dalmatian lounged by the fireplace, yawning contentedly.

"But you reported Benny missing. Could you tell me a bit more about that?" Fredrik began.

Claire's phone buzzed, and she apologized. "Yes, I did. We have had some contact since our parents are no longer around. It was mostly messages. I hadn't heard from him in a while, but then I received a reminder about an unpaid electricity bill—his apartment is in my name. I sent him a message on March twenty-third, but he never replied. I even tried calling once, but there was no answer." She recounted this as though it were a chore.

"You had a key to his apartment, then?"

"That's right. Benny rented the apartment from me for a while when things were a bit rough for him. He had no family of his own, you know. Always broke, always spending too much." She laughed lightly, brushing back her hair.

"And how would you describe Benny? Who were his closest friends?"

"Friends? I'm not sure he had any. He mostly kept to himself and his cameras, but that didn't help him much. He was a dreamer—an underdog, I suppose. He never really made it."

"Any enemies or bad habits? Anyone who might have wanted to harm him?"

Fredrik struggled to maintain his patience. Claire showed little concern, almost disdain, for her brother's life. Unlike most family members, who would press for answers, Claire didn't seem to have a single question about Benny's death.

"Not really. I've heard he'd go out drinking every other night, but I didn't track his every move, did I? I have my own life and family to worry about. I know he borrowed money here and there, but… small towns are always full of gossip, aren't they?" She laughed, the sound bordering on dismissiveness.

"I see. And you didn't share his interest in photography?"

"Not at all," she replied, gesturing toward the paintings on the walls. "I prefer real art, as you can see. Anyone can snap a photo. However, a brushstroke takes real precision and skill."

Claire made a sweeping gesture in front of an abstract painting. Fredrik couldn't determine whether it was impressive, genuine, or expensive, but Claire appeared to know her art. She put her phone on a cluttered side table and picked up another painting.

"This is mixed media," she explained. "And, no, it's not a copy; there are limits to what I'd do."

The painting was a chaotic blend of graffiti, cut-out newspaper articles, fabric scraps, photo fragments, and marker scrawls. Fredrik's first thought was that a child could have made it.

"How much does something like this go for?" he asked.

"This one's called Spring Hope, and I'm selling it for fifteen thousand euros."

"I see. When did you last see Benny? Did he seem different in any way?"

"Not really. He mostly talked about his car, the Ferrari. It was a bit sad, actually, driving around in that thing while barely managing to pay rent."

As their conversation wound down, Claire extended an invitation to her upcoming exhibition. Fredrik accepted politely but felt he'd learn more from a brick wall.

As he pulled away from her curated life, his phone buzzed with a message from an unknown number.

The fun has just begun. You bastard.

In the rearview mirror, he saw Claire stepping onto her elegant, glass-covered veranda. *How vastly different people could be,* he thought.

* * *

It was nearly four o'clock when Fredrik received news that Moa and Erik were heading back and wanted a quick meeting. He called Grim, who mentioned he had new information, and they arranged to meet in the staff restaurant.

The aroma of food made Fredrik's stomach rumble—he'd skipped lunch.

"You mentioned the lasagna. Should I try it?" he asked Grim.

"You won't regret it," he replied with a grin. "You'll be thanking me later."

The staff restaurant at the police station in Stockholm felt more like a school canteen and couldn't compare to The Vault. It offered large windows and plenty of greenery, adding an extra stress relief layer. The aroma suggested that the food could compete with a few Michelin-star dishes.

"This is what'll keep you going," Erik said, taking another bite. "If you're going to last a good forty-five years on the job, you need decent food and a quiet corner to recharge."

"Amen to that." Moa laughed.

"Claire and Benny were like day and night," Fredrik said, his mind drifting to his sons, who had been so different. "Being siblings doesn't mean you're alike."

He thought of Ronny, his lively and outgoing son, who seemed to have everything under control until he didn't and ended his life. And Dennis, the introspective academic pursuing art in Amsterdam. Two boys raised with the same love and opportunities, yet so different.

"To sum up Benny, I'd say he was passionate about his photography, detail-oriented, but perhaps a bit… lacking," Erik added. "His apartment was messy. Maybe he didn't care because it wasn't his, but his camera equipment was pristine."

"I checked his finances," Grim said. "His business was struggling. According to his accountant, his expenses consistently outweighed his income."

"Was he holding out for a big break?" Moa suggested.

"Could be. It might explain his obsession with suing Claire. But considering the high legal fees and low income from his photos, it hardly seemed worthwhile."

"Sometimes siblings don't make sense," Erik said, sipping his water. "But he definitely valued his equipment. His camera cabinet was full, and each camera was boxed with receipts. Nothing was stolen."

"Have you received the call logs yet?" Fredrik asked Grim.

"They're on the way. There was a mix-up, and another case got prioritized, but we should have them soon."

Fredrik's ex-wife called. A fleeting thought crossed his mind: could she be the one sending him those anonymous messages?

CHAPTER FOURTEEN

CAPITANOS PULLED his hat low to shield himself from the biting wind slicing through his jacket. Only a few more years of this, and then he'd sail to warmer shores, leaving the rat race far behind.

Raising his binoculars, he surveyed the scene. To the left, he spotted the lifeless body of someone who, in his mind, didn't deserve to live. The world needed stronger people who could think smarter, not just work harder. He believed the weak would ultimately be forced out of the game. He placed a hand over the silencer in his pocket—his best investment.

"Too many questions, too much morality over meaningless things," he muttered before changing his shoes and sliding into the car. Pulling a bottle of Black Label from his pocket, he took a swig, savoring the warmth spreading as he mentally scrolled through his list of trusted contacts. Not keen on handling the next job himself, he dialed a number. A faint voice answered.

"Yes?"

"Are you available next week? Another delivery."

There was a pause at the other end. Capitano's patience snapped as he slammed a fist on the steering wheel. "Available? Yes or no?"

"I'm abroad."

The line went dead.

"Damn."

A couple of seagulls circled the body, and a surge of adrenaline rushed through him. Soon, the birds would start picking at the remains. He chuckled, took another swig, and eased the car onto the road, heading toward town. He'd take care of the job himself.

CHAPTER FIFTEEN

AS FREDRIK STEPPED out of the shower, a sharp knock on the door startled him. He swore and grabbed his robe.

"Sign here," said the delivery guy, thrusting a stack of pizza boxes toward Fredrik. His cap was pulled low over his eyes, and loud music blared from his headphones.

"I didn't order anything," Fredrik protested.

"Just sign," the delivery guy repeated, louder this time, tapping his foot impatiently.

Fredrik signed and placed the boxes on the table. Wet footprints dotted the floor, and he cursed under his breath. He was already running late for his date with Moa. He briefly considered taking the pizzas to Hanna at the pub—maybe they could freeze them or give them away. But he quickly dismissed the idea, realizing it would lead to questions he didn't want to answer. He thought about calling his ex-wife to vent, but opted to get dressed and leave the pizzas behind. At least the room would smell inviting when he returned. He'd dispose of the boxes later when no one was around.

"Hi," Ingrid said, taking the final step on the stairs.

"Hi there, so we're neighbors. Nice." He fumbled for words, checking his watch. "Sorry, I'm in a hurry, but I'll catch up with you later, alright?"

He felt a pang of guilt for being so abrupt. Ingrid had suffered a serious fall from her former life of luxury, now living in a studio apartment and working at the pub. He vowed to say something kind to her next time.

The back door of the pub creaked as Fredrik slipped inside. He hoped to spot Tore, gauge his mood, and see if he could bring up the mysterious man with pointed ears he'd seen him with the other day.

"Has Tore been around today?" he asked Hanna, who was lining up glasses on a shelf.

"Not today or last night," Hanna replied, glancing up. "So, he's probably on his way. Going out? I thought you were having a party—the delivery guy assumed all those pizzas were for the pub."

Fredrik forced a laugh, his mind racing. "They're, um, coming later," he lied, stepping out onto the street.

* * *

"Cheers," Moa said, raising her glass and smiling. "Welcome home."

Fredrik felt relaxed. The strange messages, the suspicions about his ex-wife, and the peculiar delivery of ten pizzas faded away in the candlelit glow at the table. The

Loft had its charm, recommended by the Michelin Guide, with wooden tables tucked into cozy, private booths.

The entire place was illuminated solely by candlelight, as soft piano music filled the air. Handwritten menus in delicate cursive gave the place a welcoming atmosphere. The absence of modern technology was refreshing; guests were encouraged to stow their phones in small wooden boxes on each table. Fredrik already knew this would become his and Moa's regular spot.

"Even though I haven't explored all the islands yet, it's already starting to feel like home here," Fredrik said, setting down his glass. "Stockholm is a closed chapter for me now; I'll return only as a tourist. So… How are you doing?"

Moa set down her glass. "Well, things have been chaotic, to say the least."

She gave him a brief update on Tomas's accident and her mother's health. "It's exhausting, both physically and financially. But I'm managing. I have to."

Fredrik didn't want to add to her worries and decided to ask Grim later if there was a way to track the hidden number that sent the messages.

"I had a quick chat with Ingrid. Considering everything she's been through, she seems to be holding up," he said.

"Most of us are stronger than we realize," Moa replied, smiling softly. "But what about your summer cottage in Nordby? Are you renting it out?"

"Yes. After repairing the water damage, I finally set it up as a rental. After the fire and my divorce, I stayed on the mainland longer than planned to sort out the insurance claim. Eventually, I crashed with friends and added a few courses to my CV. But now I'm here, ready for a new chapter."

Fredrik was eager to put it all behind him: his wife burning down their villa and finally getting the divorce papers signed.

"You look beautiful. Green suits you," he said impulsively, watching Moa's cheeks turn pink.

"Thank you. I've missed you, Fredrik. But as I said, it's been so hectic. Let's keep things casual for a while and meet up whenever we can find some time. You mentioned Dennis might come to visit this summer?"

"Yes, he'll have his summer break, and I'll take a few days off—my first proper vacation in a long time. Maybe we could stay at my cottage and be tourists for a while. I hear the islands have many festivals during the summer. Do you suggest any particular time in mind for taking vacation leave?"

"Around mid-July to the end of the month; the Friland Summer Festival will be in full swing then," she said. "It's a great time for visitors with all the performances, but for us, it can be an exhausting period—lots of hassles, drunks, and fights," Moa warned, her eyes twinkling with humor.

"Thanks for the heads-up, but I think I'll manage. I noticed there's a carnival in March. Is there anything I should know?"

"Oh, that's the Ostara Carnival in March," Moa explained. "It's our spring celebration, though it usually rains. The main streets in the larger towns are packed with parades and people in costumes. There's some litter and a few drunks, but overall, it's a fun time. What's your take on Claire?"

"Let's just say she's nothing like her brother, even though I didn't know him," Fredrik replied with a grin. "I didn't quite get a read on her, but my gut tells me she's worth keeping an eye on."

CHAPTER SIXTEEN

THERE WERE NOT ENOUGH hours in the day. After work, Moa had to stop by her brother Tomas's place with a fresh cap and new clothes. The Sweaty and Dissatisfied often criticized any outfit that wasn't effortless to slip on and off, as if the caregiver's convenience mattered more than Tomas's comfort. She hated seeing him in sweatpants day after day. Moa wanted him to feel the difference between daywear and nightwear. But The Sweaty and Dissatisfied despised buttons and zippers. She probably resented Moa for taking his clothes home, washing and ironing them, and still balancing a regular job and gym routine. Moa almost enjoyed pushing the buttons of people like her, who preferred complaining about every minor inconvenience rather than considering ways to improve things for the residents. Fortunately, the rest of the staff seemed to understand how vital it was for residents to feel a sense of dignity and care.

Moa's mom was in good hands for now; an assistant would escort her to the podiatrist and hairdresser, and Kajsa had promised to bring her back to the house to spend the night—likely the last time in her own home. Kajsa was Moa's guardian angel, but even angels came at a price. As Moa tucked her phone away, it buzzed with a message from the unit manager at Tomas's rehabilitation center.

You are requested to attend a meeting on Friday at six o'clock in the evening. We must discuss how the municipality's budget cuts will impact the residents.

Moa set her phone down and counted to ten. She refused to lose her patience—this was out of her control. Life went on, things fell apart, and she had to find a way to manage, but no more than that.

She turned her attention to the computer and pulled up the lab report on the cups collected from Benny's apartment. The results indicated that a visitor had left traces—fingerprints and a small amount of DNA—but they didn't match anything in the database.

Moa took a sip of water and forwarded the update to Fredrik. Considering the disarray in parts of the apartment, the visitor who shared coffee with Benny was likely there many days, if not weeks, before he vanished.

She called Vilda, who answered immediately.

"I'll meet you outside in five minutes," she said. "The usual place."

Moa tucked her phone away again, feeling the weight of the favor she owed Vilda.

The north wind tugged at her jacket as Moa approached the bench outside the police station, their regular meeting spot. Although Vilda was a private investigator and technically on the same side of the law, they had a strict policy: no work-related discussions over the phone or through messages.

"Glad you could make it. You know I wouldn't ask unless necessary," Vilda said, her knitted beanie pulled low over her ears as she blew her nose.

"Got a cold?" Moa asked, raising an eyebrow.

Vilda chuckled. "I blame my client, not a freezing stakeout. How are you? The last time we met was entertaining."

Moa laughed, remembering how Vilda had helped her handle an extortionist. "Yeah, it was. So, what's up? Do you need money?"

"Not this time. I was hoping for information. Anything you might know about the lawyer Jake Lund. I checked him out through my sources, and he's clean, of course. But if you come across anything suspicious, let me know."

"Can I ask why? Is he a client?"

Jake wasn't involved in the recent case, only assisting the police. Still, she'd have to tread carefully.

"It's the usual: his wife thinks he's cheating. She says he's acting strangely, staying out late, coming home smelling of alcohol, and his clothes are sometimes damp. She can't make sense of it."

Moa chuckled. "Not exactly unusual behavior for most men."

Vilda blew her nose and popped a lozenge. "Just keep an eye out, that's all."

"Will do. We could use more officers like you. Ever think of coming back? You were one of the best."

Vilda shook her head, sniffling in response.

Moa returned to the station, catching sight of a janitor by the elevator. She dialed Fredrik's number.

"Did you get the lab report I sent you?" she asked.

"Thanks. I'm swamped right now, but any updates?"

Moa hesitated, unsure if she was interrupting, but she recognized that even small details could be critical. "Not much, but if you're planning to talk to Jake Lund, there's a rumor that he's coming home late, smelling like he's been drinking."

"Good to know. I'll be sure to talk to him. He's got quite a network—maybe he'll have some useful information for us."

CHAPTER SEVENTEEN

FREDRIK'S OFFICE WAS finally taking shape, everything in its place. He turned down the volume on the police radio as Grim pulled out a chair and settled in.

"There's something oddly satisfying about listening to those calls, right?"

Grim said, "It took me a while to get used to not rushing out every time a call came. But I've come to terms with it. I'm just as useful here in the office. Have you settled into the routines?"

Fredrik set down the pen he'd been absently spinning—a habit he needed to break.

"Faster than I expected. But sometimes, I miss the excitement of arriving at a scene and uncovering critical evidence."

Grim clasped his hands behind his head, stretching.

"Trust me, you'll get your adrenaline rush here, too. The islands might seem quiet, but they're not always."

Fredrik considered asking Grim about tracking unknown numbers, but decided to wait. Bringing up a stalker in his first week might not create the best impression. Grim pulled a paper from the stack on the desk.

"I've gathered some interesting information for you. For starters, Benny booked a round-trip ferry ticket from Toft to Breda Island on February twenty-fifth but only used the outbound ticket. Since there's only one ferry line, if he left, it wasn't by ferry; he likely took a private boat and left the car behind.

"According to the missing person report, Benny used his card on February twenty-fourth to pay for the ferry. It doesn't seem like a planned trip. Was he meeting someone at the last minute?"

"Possibly. He made several short calls to Tore Viklund, the sailor, but the last call on the twenty-fifth went unanswered. He was also in regular contact with his lawyer, Jake Lund, until January. Regarding his sister Claire, he had several heated email exchanges with her. You'll find those in the attachments. Lastly, Benny sent multiple messages to Sven Stark, the security manager on the oil platform."

Fredrik skimmed through Grim's report, noting that Benny had tried to arrange a face-to-face meeting with Sven, but he had declined due to his busy schedule.

"Benny's last call to Claire was in early January and lasted over three minutes," Grim continued. "But what's interesting is his search history—appendix three. He repeatedly searched for a man named Rune Ek and his yacht business. Rune's headquarters are in Breda, with offices in Toft. I don't have all the information from Benny's devices yet, but it seems he was onto something."

"Good work. I'll wait for more details."

Fredrik dialed Tore's number and let it ring ten times before sending a follow-up message. The familiar surge of adrenaline hit him—several loose ends were waiting to be tied up.

Hanna called, asking if he could stop by his room to sign for an urgent delivery that couldn't be left unattended. Fredrik hadn't ordered anything, but since he was already heading toward Jake's office nearby, he decided to make the stop.

Arriving at his room, Fredrik cursed as the delivery guy handed over a heavy package. Inside, there were three pet urns. He searched for a packing slip or a sender, confident he could trace the order, but found none. He shoved the box under the bed and carefully locked the door.

As he stepped onto the street, his phone lit up with a new message. Despite his thick down jacket, he shivered as he read it.

Everyone will soon find out what an idiot you are.

The message wasn't threatening; it was merely unsettling and childish. As he entered Jake Lund's office, more notifications flooded his screen. He counted twenty messages before finally silencing his phone.

CHAPTER EIGHTEEN

A FRIENDLY RECEPTIONIST welcomed Fredrik. Two green Chesterfield sofas dominated the reception area of Jake Lund's office, while the walls were adorned with paintings of English hunting scenes. Magazines like *Forbes*, *The Economist*, and several luxury yacht publications were neatly arranged on the coffee table. A tall, well-built, middle-aged man in a black suit and shiny shoes smiled confidently at Fredrik. His attire complemented the decor far better than Fredrik's jeans, sneakers, and ketchup-stained jacket.

"Jake Lund. This morning, I heard on the news that it's confirmed to be Benny. Please, take a seat," he said, gesturing to a smaller seating area in front of his desk.

"Coffee?"

Without waiting for a response, he pressed a button on a sleek coffee machine and handed Fredrik a steaming cup of black coffee.

"What can I do for you?"

"I understand that Benny Palm hired you to manage a legal dispute with his sister. I hope you can provide some information about him. When did you last see him?"

"It was in early January. Benny won the case, and Claire was ordered to pay a settlement."

As if reading Fredrik's thoughts, Jake said, "But she had no reason to kill him. The settlement was small, and the case was tricky and complicated."

Fredrik sipped his bitter, overly pungent coffee. He felt his phone vibrating in his pocket with new messages.

"Do you know if anyone wanted to harm Benny?"

Jake shook his head.

"He was obsessed with photography."

"How would you describe Claire?"

"I know who she is. On such a small island, people know everything about each other and invent what they don't know. There are many unpleasant rumors about her, but I hope they're just gossip. She's like most of us, trying to make a decent living. Unfortunately, she takes many shortcuts and produces an enormous amount in a short time. But as I mentioned, she's a harmless person. From what I understand, they've avoided each other. So, are you new to the islands? I detect a slight accent."

"That's right. I'm from the mainland."

"Many digital nomads are flocking to the islands, and I wouldn't be surprised if there's an increase in organized crime. Yesterday, I received fifteen inquiries about the easiest ways to start a business here, tax regulations, and more. The new generation is looking for some sort of starter pack and doesn't realize how much work is involved. As I mentioned, Benny lived for his photos; he called it art. His finances were unstable. I don't usually offer payment plans, but I sympathized with him. Perhaps he had debts?"

A knock echoed at the door.

"Your wife is on the phone. She said it was important," the secretary informed.

Jake excused himself. Fredrik caught snippets of soothing words, reminiscent of what he had once said to his ex-wife.

"Apologies for that. My wife suffers from anxiety paired with a severe cold."

"I've heard you're in the recycling business?"

"Yes, I recycle tires from companies across Scandinavia. The tires are ground into chips and used as building materials and flooring in Senegal. I hire individuals looking to re-enter the workforce, and it feels rewarding to give something back. The surplus funds a school in Senegal. My wife is also involved in the project, Tires of Hope."

"How do you transport everything to Senegal?"

"Everything ships via cargo vessels, both incoming and outgoing. If you're interested, I can show you our facility in the old port, but we'd need to arrange an appointment."

"That would be great."

Fredrik realized there was nothing more to gain from Jake Lund, thanked him, and stood up. A few framed photos caught his eye on a small bookshelf. One photo showed Jake smiling next to a man with pointed ears. They were on a boat under a clear blue sky, the sun shining brightly behind them.

"So, you know each other?" Fredrik probed, hoping Jake would take the bait.

"Yes, everyone knows Rune. We do business together. He's a really good guy. Like most people here on the islands, he's also involved in the boat industry."

Jake handed Fredrik a black business card with gold print: *Rune Ek – Yachts & Moore.*

"If you ever fancy a day out, charter a yacht with a crew."

He laughed, and Fredrik smiled. A day on one of Rune's boats would likely cost a police officer an entire month's salary.

On his way to the station, Fredrik checked his phone and found 311 messages.

Moa and Erik waited for a brief meeting at the station. He looked forward to talking with sensible people who remained grounded. His phone kept filling with messages. He had never had a stalker before and was not eager to deal with the situation.

CHAPTER NINETEEN

MOA'S GAZE LINGERED on the noticeboard as it gradually filled with notes and pictures, slowly piecing together the story of the case. Erik, standing nearby, took off his glasses and rubbed his tired eyes.

"Headache?" Moa asked, glancing in his direction.

"Yeah," he sighed. "Probably from lack of sleep. My eldest recently became a teenager and thought coming home way too late last night was acceptable. I was up most of the night, imagining every worst-case scenario."

Moa understood. She, too, had spent sleepless nights, her mind trapped in a relentless cycle of worst-case scenarios playing over and over. A faint glimmer of relief sparked when Fredrik walked into the room, his presence carrying a sense of steadiness. Everyone had their battles, she thought, but Fredrik had a way of keeping his struggles firmly in the rearview mirror.

"Grim's on his way," Fredrik said as he placed a stack of papers on the table. "He got stuck helping a colleague with a slow laptop."

Erik chuckled dryly, slipping his glasses back on. "I don't envy him. Always being the tech guy—he must be exhausted."

Fredrik shrugged off his jacket, draped it over a chair, and arranged his papers. He turned off his phone and pinned a new note to the board. Grim entered moments later, shaking his head.

"Sorry," Grim said as he dropped into a seat. "I've become IT support wherever I go. Setting boundaries without seeming rude? Still working on that."

Fredrik tapped the newly added note on the board.

"I've sent a patrol to the port in Breda to ask if anyone has spotted Benny. His car is hard to miss. We are waiting for the security footage from the port to confirm whether he was alone in the car. Oh, and Claire mentioned something about financial troubles. Grim, do you have any up dates on that?"

"He lived beyond his means," Fredrik said. "He bought a lot on credit, spent heavily when he had money, and scraped by when he didn't. We found receipts from the photo store near the square—might be worth checking out."

"Good idea," Moa remarked.

"I'll put a question mark next to Benny's sister, Claire. Grim, can you run a background check on her?"

Grim noted it, and Moa redirected her attention. "What about Jake? Did he provide us with anything useful for the investigation?"

Fredrik said, "Jake suggested Benny might have had debts and would get back to me if he could think of anything to help us. Jake seems hardworking and invited me to tour his recycling project. His wife is also involved in their charity, Tires of Hope. They appear to be doing well, but he mentioned that she suffers from anxiety, so she is having a break from the project. Once we receive the maritime police report, we can investigate any ships that passed through the area where Benny was found. Oh, and Jake has a colleague named Rune Ek. I saw Rune with Tore at The Norse Inn. I've tried to contact Tore, but I had no luck. I'm sure I saw Rune in one of Benny's photos."

Fredrik pinned a photo of Rune on the noticeboard and turned to Moa and Erik. Moa continued, "Benny had a visitor in his apartment. They shared coffee, but we haven't yet matched the small amount of DNA left on the cup. The same goes for the limited fingerprints we found—no matches. However, we discovered another phone among Benny's belongings. There's a clear image of another warehouse on it, and I swear, this one looks familiar."

Moa pulled out the photo, her finger resting on a section of a faded poster from an ice cream stand in the background. "Doesn't that look like the one near Jake's warehouse? The spot where we stored the Ferrari?"

"Good catch," Fredrik replied. "I'll check it out. I'm meeting Sven in Toft soon—Benny has called him several times to arrange a meeting. I'll also stop by that photo store on my way back."

Late afternoon sunlight streamed through the windows as they wrapped up the meeting. Moa lingered, hesitant to return home to the reality of her unraveling life. Work felt more effortless, but it was a distraction she wasn't ready to let go of. "Mind if I tag along?" she asked Fredrik.

He smirked. "Quality time together? Sure. I want to tie up as many loose ends as possible before the day's over."

Moa knew she would be on call all night with little chance of rest. Helping Fredrik for a couple of hours seemed like a better use of her time.

* * *

At the café in Toft, Sven waited, perched stiffly at a table, drumming his fingers and scrolling on his phone. He glanced up as they approached.

"Glad you could make it," Fredrik said, offering his hand. "I'm Fredrik, and I believe you've met Moa before. Thanks for taking the time. I know you're busy."

Sven's gaze lingered on Moa a second too long, making her regret the decision to come along.

"Yeah, it's hectic," Sven said, shaking Fredrik's hand. "You caught me in town by chance. I heard this is about that photographer who was found dead."

"That's right," Fredrik confirmed. "Benny contacted you several times—calls, messages. Do you know what he wanted?"

"He wanted to talk, but I didn't have the time. I assumed it was to get permission to photograph the platform. We always have photographers and vloggers in Torshamn chasing shots of the rig against the northern lights. Those illuminated masts have become a trend. However, many areas are restricted, and we've been a bit too lenient with permits."

Sven launched into a monologue about safety protocols, legal requirements, and the courses he had taken, his tone bordering on self-importance. He appeared more interested in discussing himself than in offering help.

Moa glanced at Fredrik, who was tuning out Sven's ramblings, his focus on the case instead. Her thoughts drifted. Was there a connection between the warehouses, the boats, and the oil platform—something Benny was pursuing? Perhaps he was chasing the perfect shot? A photograph that could win a competition, garner recognition, or provide a financial lifeline?

CHAPTER TWENTY

FREDRIK HAD OVER 500 unread messages on his phone. He wouldn't be able to relax without calling his ex-wife and asking her to stop the relentless harassment.

"I get the feeling Sven was more interested in showing off his expertise than helping us," Fredrik said as he walked alongside Moa toward the square in Toft. He paused, studying her. "Are you okay? You look a bit pale."

"Just a headache, probably from lack of sleep," Moa replied. "But don't you think it's strange? Sven was at the site when Benny's body was discovered—the very person Benny had been trying so hard to contact."

Fredrik agreed; his expression reflective. "Fate has a cruel sense of humor. You should head home to rest. If you get called out, it will be a long night."

"It's fine," Moa replied, dismissing the concern. "I have a feeling it'll be a quiet night. I'll catch up on sleep later."

As they approached the photo store, Fredrik sent a quick message to Grim. A small bell chimed when he pushed the door open, echoing with nostalgic charm. The interior appeared to have been plucked straight from the nineties.

A young woman stood behind the counter, her tattoos and piercings vividly contrasting with the store's outdated decor. She greeted them with a warm smile. Fredrik displayed his badge.

"It's about Benny, isn't it?"

"Unfortunately, yes," Fredrik said. "We understand he was a regular here?"

"Benny was our best customer," the girl replied, her voice tinged with sadness. "He was always kind and seemed to know so much. He came in about once a month to drop off color films for development and would buy photo paper and chemicals. It's so awful."

"Did you notice anything unusual about him? When was the last time you saw him? Anything that might help us in the investigation?"

The girl shook her head, her eyes glistening with unshed tears. "He was easy to talk to, you know. We'd chat about angles and light—things no one else understands. He made everything sound so fascinating."

Fredrik flipped open his notebook and began jotting down details. The air in the shop was thick with the rich scent of paper and film-developing chemicals, a lingering relic of another era.

"And Benny always paid upfront," the girl added. "That's rare. Most of our regulars pay by invoice, and we're constantly chasing them for payment."

Fredrik closed his notebook. They thanked her and stepped onto the street, but she poked her head out before the door shut behind them.

"Wait," she called, her voice urgent. "I remembered something. One of the last things Benny said was that he was onto something big. I don't know what he meant, but it seemed important."

Fredrik exchanged a glance with Moa. "Thank you," he said. "That's helpful."

* * *

Rune Ek led them into a cluttered room filled with boxes, muttering an apology. He explained that he was in the process of setting up a small office in the old port, although he primarily worked on Breda Island, where the head office was located.

There was no doubt—this was the same man from the photo on Benny's camera. His pointed ears and sharp features made him stand out next to Jake Lund, Friland's most astute lawyer.

"How can I help you?" Rune asked, brushing dust off his jacket.

"We're investigating Benny Palm, the photographer who was recently found dead," Fredrik said, showing him a picture. "Your office is near the photo store he frequently visited."

Rune frowned, his eyes narrowing as he glanced at the image. Then he shook his head. "Sorry, I don't recognize him. I've never seen him before."

Fredrik sensed the need for a different approach. "Are you mooring yachts here in Toft, too?" he asked.

Rune yanked a piece of tape from a box, tossing it into a corner with a frustrated flick.

"Yes. I manage operations from the old port and plan to station a few more yachts there permanently."

"Do you know Tore Viklund?" Fredrik continued.

Rune's tone shifted, becoming almost reverent.

"He's one of my best seamen. Always available for last-minute bookings and knows the waters around Friland better than anyone. He's been in this business for decades."

Rune's phone buzzed, and he excused himself. Fredrik used the break to check his messages. Grim had sent a text confirming that Rune Ek's company rented a warehouse in the old port next to Jake Lund's. It was likely near the ice cream stand poster seen in Benny's photo. Fredrik made a mental note to verify it before the night was over.

Moa stood silently, blinking and shivering slightly in the cool air. Rune returned, ending the conversation with a curt, "Anything else?"

"No, thank you," Fredrik replied. "We'll follow up if we need more information."

As they walked out, Fredrik's thoughts lingered on Tore. If anyone could explain how to sink a Ferrari into the sea, it would be him. Pulling out his phone, Fredrik redialed Tore's number. The phone rang ten times before going to voicemail. He left a message, informing Tore that he was on his way. After all, Tore's four decades of experience working on boats made him the best bet for understanding what type of vessel might be linked to the discovery site. Still, it felt like searching for a needle in a haystack.

Back in the car, Moa zipped up her jacket, yawning as she said, "Rune's hiding something, and Tore knows about it. Benny stumbled upon their secret, didn't he?"

A faint smile was tugging at the corner of Fredrik's mouth. "That seems about right. It's a good starting point."

"But could you load a Ferrari onto a yacht?" she asked.

"With a large enough yacht, yes. It is possible."

Fredrik slowed the car as they approached the dimly lit warehouses. A flickering streetlamp cast a weak, pale light over the area. It was nearly eight in the evening.

"That's definitely the same poster," Moa said, holding up the photo from Benny's phone. "And it matches the address Grim sent."

Fredrik leaned back in his seat, glancing at her. "How about we grab a bite at The Norse Inn before calling it a day?"

Moa opened her mouth to respond, but her phone buzzed. She answered, her expression hardening as she listened. Then, grimacing, she ended the call.

"A body has been found near the cliffs by Boda Lighthouse," she said, her tone sharp. "Rescue services are on their way. A witness stumbled right onto it, and apparently, the body was badly decomposed. Erik has requested additional forensic experts, and two patrols are already there. I need to go."

"Be careful."

CHAPTER TWENTY-ONE

THE WAVES POUNDED relentlessly against the cliffs, creating a deafening symphony of chaos. Moa was back at the same spot where she had been a few days earlier. Back then, she had felt exhausted, alone, and lost, with the lighthouse's steady blinking offering no sliver of hope or security. Tonight, she felt weary but was surrounded by colleagues, and her presence was essential. She was needed and grateful to be alive.

The body was discovered only meters from the cliff's edge. Floodlights illuminated the scene with harsh intensity, while the lighthouse's fleeting flashes added an eerie rhythm to the unfolding investigation.

"She's only fifteen," a patrolling officer said, his voice heavy as he began to string barricade tape. Panicked cries and distressed voices from the ambulance cut through the bitter night air.

"What the hell was she doing out here in the dark?" Moa asked, her voice barely containing frustration.

The officer shrugged helplessly. "Apparently, it's some TikTok thing—a trend called Dark Dare. Kids run full speed through unfamiliar places in the dark to confront their fears. We tried to persuade her to hand over her phone, but she's not cooperating yet. She was livestreaming when she fell."

He secured the barricade tape to a bush, his movements tense, then gestured toward the ambulance. "She's in shock. Her face... It's full of maggots and debris. She went down headfirst."

Moa grimaced. "Wait here," she told Erik, striding toward the ambulance as the harsh north wind bit at her face. The body lay nearby, bloated and beginning to decompose, foam seeping from the nose and mouth. It had likely been there for days. The chances of uncovering fresh evidence were slim—unless the killer had returned to the scene, a possibility that lingered in the back of Moa's mind.

"We'll need you to bag everything," she instructed the paramedics. "Blankets, sheets, her clothes—anything that has been in contact with her. Please send it to us as soon as possible. How is she holding up?"

One of the paramedics looked up, his face tense. "She is getting more restless and disoriented. Her face is smeared with debris, and she is struggling. We are starting her on an IV of antibiotics immediately."

"We'll send a patrol to the ER to monitor anyone who shows up. The last thing we need is for the press to catch wind of this. We also need her phone—somehow—and we'll track down her relatives."

The night stretched ahead, heavy with questions and the bitter taste of tragedy. The nurse nodded as if he'd heard the same request hundreds of times before. His calm demeanor suggested that, for the investigators, every case held the same level of urgency. For this, Moa was grateful.

"No problem."

* * *

Moa and Erik stood silently by the dead body for a few minutes, gathering their thoughts. This quiet moment was a ritual, a way to honor the victim and mentally prepare for the methodical work ahead.

"A shot to the forehead," Erik said, breaking the silence. "Bullseye. Likely someone he knew. Close range?"

"Probably. It appears to be a nine-millimeter." Moa crouched closer, pointing at the back of the man's hand. "Do you see the tattoo? It looks homemade."

An anchor entwined with a heart marked his left hand.

"Tore?" Erik asked. "The regular at The Norse Inn?"

Their suspicions were confirmed during the search when they discovered Tore Vikholm's wallet, driver's license, and phone. Moa and Erik carefully bagged his belongings as evidence and labeled them, working in sync until the forensic pathologist, Ida, arrived. She examined the body, her expression grim.

"The body's been here a few days," she confirmed. "Wind, weather, and birds have taken their toll, causing significant damage. Fish bones," she added, stepping back from the swollen, decomposed face. "See them lodged there?"

"The birds," Erik said, grimacing. "It's as if they knew what they were doing."

"Have you found the bullet?" Ida asked.

"Not yet," Moa replied. "We've requested a K-9 unit to help."

The ambulance and a patrol car left the scene.

"It seems he has paint under his nails," Moa noted. "How did he even get here? It's at least two kilometers from the nearest house. Did the patrol report any tire tracks?"

Erik said, "Yeah, two sets. The sooner we get him moved, the better."

Moa shivered, pulling out her phone to call Fredrik, who had left earlier after a quick survey of the scene.

"Any updates?" he asked.

"It's looking like a close-range execution-style shot to the forehead," Moa said. "We found fish bones embedded in his face. The victim is most likely Tore Vikholm. We found his driver's license."

Fredrik's sigh was audible over the line. "Damn."

"Exactly."

By half-past five in the morning, Moa and Erik returned to Toft. Erik drove the van through the empty streets, eyes scanning the desolate town. A string of numbers had been hastily scrawled near the garage entrance at the police station.

"It won't be long before we have graffiti inside the corridors," Erik joked. "Has Fredrik contacted us? I assume he's been working all night."

Moa smiled. "Nope," she replied. "He wants us to get a couple of hours of sleep—it's an order. And he managed to get some rest himself."

"That sounds wise."

The harsh, raw world outside seemed to fade as the van rolled into the illuminated garage. Moa had no intention of heading into the office. She would unpack the items that needed processing, leave instructions for her colleagues, and then go straight to bed. She needed to recharge for the endless grind of a career that would extend for another thirty years.

* * *

At the usual meeting spot, Vilda was waiting, phone in hand. Moa approached her without hesitation, knowing it was better to deal with it immediately.

"I don't have much time today," Moa said. "We just got back. Jake mentioned that his wife is feeling nervous—something about bad nerves. That's all I have for now."

Vilda sniffled, blowing her nose. "I've been careless," she said, her voice trembling. "Someone's started blackmailing me. I need money. Please don't contact me until I give the go-ahead. I hope I can rely on you."

CHAPTER TWENTY-TWO

FREDRIK FELT THE PULL to stay up all night, diving headfirst into unraveling Tore's life. His shoulder, which had begun aching again, was a sharp reminder to pace himself.

When he arrived at the meeting room, Moa and Erik were already waiting, their expressions focused. Grim, true to form, was running a few minutes late. Fredrik pinned a picture of Tore on the noticeboard. He turned to the group and said, "We've got some updates from the lab. Tore's DNA was found on a cup in Benny's apartment, confirming a direct connection between the two. As for the stone found in Benny's car, it's polished limestone—a common material in nearly every other garden here on the islands."

Fredrik scanned the room, waiting for anyone to offer answers or theories. "And here's the kicker: Benny had traces of cocaine in his system and was likely conscious at the time of his death. Do we know if he had a drug problem? Could that have been the root of his financial troubles? And could his death be connected? Perhaps a debt to a supplier?"

Fredrik leaned back slightly, allowing the team some space to process. "Thoughts?" he asked.

Erik shook his head in frustration while Grim jotted notes in his notebook and said, "I've reviewed the video from the port on Breda Island. It shows Benny driving ashore, which aligns with the ferry ticket. I should have the full footage by tomorrow morning. From what I've observed, Benny was alone in the car and didn't appear to interact with anyone." He glanced at Fredrik before continuing. "We've also received the passenger list from that day. My team is working on contacting everyone on it. Unfortunately, there are no cameras onboard the ferry. The crossing takes about forty-five minutes, and most people remain in their vehicles."

Fredrik clenched his jaw, silently berating himself for not reaching out to Tore sooner. "We can eliminate Sven Stark from the list of suspects," he said. "One of Benny's accounts revealed a conversation with another photographer. They discussed the upcoming meteor shower in April and May, and Benny mentioned trying to expedite the permit process by going directly through Sven."

"So, the 'big thing' Benny was onto—the one the girl at the photo store mentioned—might it be a photo?" Moa asked, her tone skeptical.

Fredrik nodded thoughtfully. "We can't rule it out. But if he uncovered something criminal, it would put him in far greater danger than chasing a shot of a meteor shower. This could go deeper."

Turning to Erik, Fredrik asked, "Do you have any news about the car?"

"We've finished our investigation but asked our colleagues to check it again to ensure we didn't miss anything."

Fredrik shifted gears. "I've been investigating Claire's recent activity. You all have the latest report in your files." He paused for a moment before continuing. "Nothing substantial so far, but we're closely watching her. She does possess a hunting license, but it's hard to imagine her shooting Tore—an experienced sailor—execution-style at close range. She's cooperating—to a degree—and we've seized her weapon. However, before jumping to conclusions, I was hoping you could review the report we received from the marine police. They've done their best to summarize it. The cargo ships pass far from the discovery site so that we can rule them out. Given the recent extreme winds, the only nearby vessels were fishing boats, many of which had to alter their planned routes because of the weather. The transponder on the involved vessel was most likely turned off when Benny and his car were dumped."

"Could it have been a helicopter?" Grim suggested.

Fredrik said, "It's a possibility I'm considering."

Moa cleared her throat and said, "Tore had a significant amount of black paint under three nails on his right hand and upon his fingertips. While that's not unusual, he might have been working on a renovation. We're leaving no stone unturned—we sent all the materials to the lab early this morning. Tomorrow, following the autopsy, we will conduct a thorough search of his house. The body was in a dreadful condition. Birds had pecked at it, and we found fish bones embedded in the face, likely placed there intentionally to attract them. It was... gruesome."

She paused before adding, "I received word from the patrol at the hospital. The girl is responding to antibiotics. She's fifteen—known on Tiktok for her daring challenges." Moa turned to Grim. "You mentioned you had something about that?"

"That's right," Grim said. "She was livestreaming when she ran out toward the cliff. Fortunately, her poor reception ended the stream before her followers could figure out where she was and search for her. She hit the camera button during the fall, which stopped the stream. The camera was in selfie mode, so nobody saw what was before her."

A heavy silence descended upon the room as everyone exchanged uneasy glances. Despite his years of experience, Fredrik felt a chill run down his spine. He took a sip of water before shattering the silence.

"Constant connectivity," he said, his voice steady yet grave. "It has its benefits, but there are also serious downsides. Unfortunately."

Fredrik called Dr. Ulrik, who seemed genuinely pleased to hear from him and promptly scheduled an appointment. The weather might have triggered the ongoing ache in Fredrik's shoulder, but he was done ignoring it. The discomfort had persisted long enough. This time, he resolved to follow all the doctor's recommendations and take any prescribed medication without protest.

As he returned home, he noticed a pizza delivery driver leaving with an empty thermal bag. The rich aroma of melted cheese and spices wafted through the stairwell, stopping him in his tracks. Ingrid had asked him to help transfer files to Dropbox, but what awaited him instead was unexpected.

Ingrid stood outside her apartment door, looking visibly flustered and clutching an armful of pizza boxes—at least ten.

"This is insane," she said, her voice laced with frustration. "I didn't order these. Is someone pranking me?"

Fredrik approached, his instincts kicking in. He immediately ruled out his ex-wife as a suspect, but the incident felt far from random. His phone buzzed furiously in his pocket just as he was about to respond. He glanced at the screen, watching a flood of new messages fill his inbox.

CHAPTER TWENTY-THREE

CAPITANOS SLOWED HIS stride, the distant wail of sirens and the flash of blue lights confirming his long-held anticipation. He had expected this moment, surprised only by how long it took for the body to be found. Around him, the world stood unnervingly still, unchanged and waiting, as if bracing for the next act in his carefully orchestrated play.

A thrill surged through him, electrifying every nerve. Killing had been disturbingly easy—far easier than he'd ever imagined. This discovery both shocked and exhilarated him, awakening a side of himself he hadn't known existed, a side he savored. In his eyes, the world was starkly divided: winners and losers. He believed life would be much simpler if everyone followed the rules and stayed in their rightful place. He pulled up a photo on his phone, zooming in on the face of the cop who had dared to delve into his private life. Killing a cop was always a gamble, but if it came to that, he wouldn't hesitate. Doubt wasn't an option; staying one step ahead was all that mattered.

CHAPTER TWENTY-FOUR

MOA WALKED PAST the sign on the door to the autopsy room. "Mortui vivos docent"—the dead teach the living. The sign suggested that there was actual life beyond the quiet, sterile halls. But what could Tore impart? Perhaps a stark lesson on trust and betrayal.

The gleaming autopsy tables demanded a harsh confrontation with reality. In this room, death was stripped of sentiment, laid bare in clinical precision—a brutal reminder of life's fragile cycle. Students often fell silent here, some retreating for fresh air as their courage crumbled beneath the weight of mortality. The air itself seemed to carry death's unseen presence. The low, droning hum of the refrigerator units seeped into the silence, deeply unsettling and conjuring vivid, haunting images of the preserved dead. It served as a stark reminder of vulnerability, compelling them to envision themselves zipped inside a body bag, stored in a cold drawer, with nothing but an identification band around their wrist.

Moa overheard Erik and Ida's murmurs as they discussed their summer vacation plans. During the dark season, they clung to any opportunity for lightheartedness. The rustle of protective clothing and the sharp scent of formalin filled the room. Pausing briefly, Moa suppressed her emotional response, fully stepping into her role as a forensic technician once more.

"He had healthy lungs; he wasn't a smoker," Ida remarked, carefully removing the lungs from the chest cavity.

Her voice held a steady monotone as she worked, a subtle shift that always accompanied her during autopsies. Her body language also changed—her movements slower, more deliberate, conveying respect and precision. She methodically removed the remaining organs, placing them in stainless steel bowls to be weighed, her motions efficient yet reverent.

"There's no doubt about the bird attacks," she remarked, examining the injured facial tissue. "He's also missing an eye. Did you find the bullet?"

"The K-9 unit found a nine-millimeter bullet, likely from a Sig Sauer, but we'll have more information once the ballistics report comes in," Erik replied.

Ida examined the entry wound, its diameter approximately seven millimeters, with the surrounding tissue contracted from the shot. "The exit wound aligns perfectly with the entry wound. Tore was tall, about six-foot-three, so unless your shooter was standing on a chair, they weren't short."

With practiced efficiency, Ida began stitching up the chest, her hands moving deftly as she completed the autopsy.

She washed her gloved hands under the tap, reached for the voice recorder, and began her report calmly and professionally: "Location, the forensic pathology station in Toft. Date, November nineteenth. Forensic technicians Moa Bakke and Erik Storm are present. After reviewing the photographs from the discovery site, the following observations are recorded: The body belongs to a male, found lying on his back. A blue ID band on the right wrist is labeled 'Tore Viklund.' A wristwatch was present on the left wrist. The clothing includes blue jeans, black sneakers, blue socks, gray underwear, and a white T-shirt. The clothing and wristwatch have been removed for further examination. The face shows significant damage, partially eaten by birds. Signs of violence include a seven-millimeter entry wound in the forehead. The deceased is estimated to be sixty-five years old."

She paused the recorder, her methodical tone contrasting sharply with the grim details of her findings and prepared to proceed with the next steps in the examination.

"The body has been exposed outdoors for a few days. The preliminary cause of death is an intracranial injury, with an open intracranial wound based on the findings. The examination concludes at eleven-thirty."

Moa and Erik arrived at The Vault and bumped into several colleagues. The noise level was comfortably low, but Moa couldn't help but notice Erik rubbing his temples again.

"You can take our seats—we're heading out with a patrol," said one of the colleagues, a young woman who appeared to be no older than twenty-five.

She moved a few plates to clear the table. Moa recognized her from the crime scene the day before.

"How are you, Erik? Should I get you some painkillers?" Moa asked, her tone light yet concerned.

"Thanks, but I'm fine," he replied. "I need some food. The air in the autopsy room was stifling, you could've cut it with a knife. They need to fix that ventilation system."

"The body was in terrible condition," the young colleague chimed in. "I'm probably not as accustomed to it as you all. Were you there for long?"

"Not really," Erik replied, stretching his neck. "We wrapped up just after five this morning."

"Good thing I'm heading to Thailand with my family for Christmas soon," she said, carefully dabbing her mouth with a napkin. Glancing at her colleague, she stacked the plates onto a tray and added, "We need to return to the old port. There's a loud demonstration we need to keep an eye on."

"Oh, what's the issue now?" Moa asked, trying to suppress a sigh. She didn't want to engage in another debate about the world's problems and injustices. For once, she wanted to pause, process everything life had thrown at her, and reflect without feeling the constant pressure to have an opinion.

"Too many boats."

Despite their fatigue, everyone burst into laughter. Erik stepped aside to let them pass.

"It's not kind to laugh," Moa said, shaking her head. "But sometimes I feel overwhelmed. I don't want my daily choices to come with so much anxiety. We need to live, recover from work, travel, and not obsess over every farmer or fisherman, maintaining employment for all, or turning off every light. And let's be honest, we need boats, don't we?"

Her words hung in the air momentarily, striking a balance between humor and the truth of their shared exhaustion.

"Yep," Erik said with a grin. "We definitely need boats—Friland wouldn't survive without them. I'll call the optician later; it might be time for new glasses."

"When was the last time you had your eyes checked?"

Erik chuckled, looking slightly sheepish, and avoided answering by shoving a forkful of lasagna into his mouth.

CHAPTER TWENTY-FIVE

INGRID PLACED THE coffee gently on the table, and Fredrik leaned in to help her unload it.

"We've got fresh Friland buns—straight from the bakery," she said with an enticing smile.

"Thanks, but I'll pass. I'd rather not pick up bad habits."

The rare luxury of a half-day off was something Fredrik cherished. It was his first official break in months. After staying up late helping Ingrid troubleshoot her laptop and tablet, he indulged in a well-deserved morning lie-in.

During their late-night session, Ingrid opened up about her struggles after Jan's passing and the relentless intrusion of the media. It still baffled Fredrik how even close family members could miss signs of drug abuse or criminal ties. Adding to her stress, Ingrid had received unsolicited deliveries, pizzas and other items she had never ordered.

As Fredrik sipped his coffee, Hanna walked by, her white apron speckled with red stains that looked unsettlingly like blood.

"I heard about Tore," she said, pausing. "It's sad. He was practically part of the furniture here. On the bright side, Ingrid seems a bit happier today. I heard you helped her out last night."

"Yes," Fredrik said, nodding thoughtfully. "Sometimes, listening is as important as asking questions. We connected in a way."

Hanna's eyes sparkled as she held out a plate piled high with Friland pastries. The rich aroma of vanilla drifted toward Fredrik, teasing his senses.

"Are you sure I can't tempt you with one?" she asked playfully.

Fredrik hesitated, but Hanna grinned and pointed to a slightly smaller bun on the plate. "This one's a bit too small to sell. It's on the house."

With a wink, she placed the pastry beside his modest slice of organic rye bread. "It's on the house," she insisted, her tone leaving no room for protest.

Fredrik couldn't help but smile as he eyed the pastry. The gesture was small, but it reminded him why he cherished moments like these.

Before he could thank her, Hanna was already flitting to another table, effortlessly juggling orders with cheerful efficiency that added to The Norse Inn's charm.

Breakfast at the Inn was a local favorite, and Fredrik couldn't deny how easily he'd slipped into its cozy rhythm. The ease of staying at the pub had made him complacent. The thought of returning to the grind—weekly grocery runs, meal prepping, and the discipline of healthy eating—felt overwhelming. Routines brought structure, sure, but they could also become a trap he wasn't eager to fall into.

With a reluctant sigh, Fredrik stepped out of the warm cocoon of the pub and into the crisp morning air. Ahead lay a visit to Dr. Ulrik, and while the appointment wasn't exactly exciting, the prospect of much-needed pain relief gave him something to look forward to.

* * *

Prosecutor Anna Vall was already seated in the meeting room when Fredrik arrived.

"I know I can't force the case forward, but I'm running out of patience," she began, her tone brisk. "Do you see any connection between Benny's death and Tore's? What about his sister, Claire? I'm not convinced we've explored her background thoroughly enough."

Without waiting for a response, Anna pressed on. "I want her detained. I'll assign one of our top interrogators to conduct the questioning."

Fredrik maintained his composure, refusing to take the bait. It wasn't the first time Anna's urgency had pushed the limits of protocol. Claire had a history of volatile social media posts, but there wasn't enough solid evidence to justify detaining her. Moreover, Claire and

Benny's relationship was far from close. With time running out, Fredrik realized they couldn't afford to make a mistake.

Anna retrieved a folder from her bag and spread it across the table. "We'll hold her for twenty-four hours and see how she reacts. Maybe that'll encourage her to cooperate," she stated decisively.

Her heels echoed sharply against the floor as she walked to the other side of the room. Fredrik stayed silent, letting Anna's words linger—timing was everything in moments like this.

* * *

Dr. Ulrik hadn't delivered the miracle cure Fredrik had anticipated. Instead of the quick cortisone injection he expected, Fredrik received a lecture about the dangers of cortisone overuse, the looming risk of osteoporosis, and the hazards of depending on daily painkillers. To worsen the situation, Ulrik gave him a prescription for positivity: keep training, think positively, practice deep breathing, and—of all things—try water aerobics in the hospital's heated pool. Fredrik pinned his hopes on the pool. This wasn't the same Ulrik he remembered from last year. Something had clearly changed.

The upbeat start to his morning took a nosedive. Feeling deflated, Fredrik headed to Grim's office.

"A quick question: would it be possible to track a prepaid card here on the islands?" Fredrik asked, stepping into the room.

Grim closed a tab on his laptop, stood up, and raised an eyebrow. "Asking for a friend?"

"Sort of."

Fredrik didn't have the energy to explain or involve Ingrid. She wasn't ready to file a report yet, and he respected her need for more time.

Grim leaned against his desk, deep in thought. "We're about to enact some new laws regarding prepaid cards. Currently, obtaining one without identification is far too easy, making them nearly impossible to track. However, by the end of the year, the police will have the authority to wiretap calls on even slight suspicion."

"Yeah, I've heard about that," Fredrik replied, a hint of impatience creeping into his voice.

Grim tilted his head, studying Fredrik with mild curiosity. "Stalker?"

Fredrik didn't answer immediately. The label felt too simplistic for the complex issues swirling in his mind. Instead, he offered a shrug and added, "And placed orders for home delivery—mostly pizza."

"If those orders were made through an app or website, the company should have IP data we can trace. If they were placed over the phone, there's a good chance they have recordings. Many businesses record calls; this is beneficial for us. Customer service competition is fierce in Friland, and software companies thrive in this environment. However, not everyone obtains the proper license for call recording. It's an extra step, and many businesses skip it. As you may have noticed, we are in a bit of a gray zone out here."

Fredrik thanked Grim and casually reminded him about the afternoon meeting with Moa and Erik.

"They're at Tore's apartment as we speak," Grim replied. "I expect we'll have more updates soon."

Fredrik reassured himself that the day would ultimately bring good news.

Grim glanced up and added, "Tell your friend to file a report if things escalate. I heard there are some sharp officers at the police station."

Fredrik chuckled at the veiled advice and returned to his office, already planning his next move.

CHAPTER TWENTY-SIX

MOA WELCOMED THE warmth radiating from the fire that Ingrid had lit. The icy November air clung to her skin while sharp, swirling snowflakes blanketed Toft.

"Maybe we'll have a white Christmas," Erik said with a laugh as he shrugged off his jacket.

"That would be wonderful," Moa replied, rubbing her hands together. "At least the snow brightens things up. We could use the light around here. Although I must admit, I'm a little jealous of the people heading to Thailand. But I'm not keen on long-haul flights."

"How are you holding up?" Erik asked, his tone softening as he tilted his head in concern.

"One day at a time. It is what it is. Work keeps me busy, and Kajsa has been a lifesaver."

"You missed Fredrik," Ingrid said as she approached their table with a confident smile. "He had a late breakfast and left a little while ago."

Ingrid paused, her gaze lingering on Moa with an uncomfortable intensity. Moa couldn't help but feel unease, as if a cold draft had swept through the room.

"He's brilliant with tech," Ingrid continued. "We stayed up late, and he was such a big help. You're lucky to have someone sharp at the station. A lot is happening these days."

Moa recalled meeting Ingrid last year in Nordby. Back then, Ingrid had been shy and reserved, a far cry from the woman standing before her now. For once, Moa struggled to find the right words, so she smiled politely as Ingrid disappeared behind the counter.

Erik raised an eyebrow at Ingrid's remark but remained focused on his lunch.

Moa found her mind drifting to Tore's villa. The thought of searching his home filled her with dread. If it turned out that he had been a hoarder, they would have no choice but to call in extra personnel. She pictured a dilapidated house cluttered with tools and half-finished renovations. Unfortunately, her instincts were rarely wrong—elderly single men often had a penchant for DIY projects. Wanting to shift the mood, she changed the subject.

"I have a friend who works at the postal sorting terminal," she began, brushing a strand of hair from her face. "She's always dreamed of becoming a police officer. Obsessed with crime series, she binge-watches and reads everything she can get her hands on. Recently, she flagged a package that turned out to be Contact, you know, the cold medicine with pseudoephedrine."

"Yes, there has been a noticeable increase in its use for producing amphetamines," Erik said. "It's a labor-intensive process—opening each capsule one by one to extract the contents—but it's clearly worth it to those involved."

"Exactly. With a kilogram of Contact, you can create amphetamines worth around three hundred thousand euros. Customs investigators flagged the package and contacted the police to track down whoever was behind it. The case inspired my friend to take evening classes to become a civilian investigator specializing in drug-related crimes."

"Good for her," Erik said. "Exchanging binge-watching TV for studying—that's commitment. I heard there's talk about starting a new drug unit. Friland is being used as a shortcut—smugglers repackage shipments here before sending them to the Norwegian and Swedish ports."

"Shall we get started with Tore's house then?"

"Let's go."

A notification caught her eye as Moa reached to put her phone in her pocket. It was a message from the unit manager at Tomas's rehabilitation facility. Her stomach sank as she read the alarming news: a twenty-five percent surge in cases—a significant increase underscoring the urgent need to keep Tomas at the center. She clenched her jaw, knowing she didn't have the energy or time to wage another battle with the authorities.

When she looked up, Erik was waiting, his face calm and steady. However, Moa's attention was drawn to the bar, where Ingrid sneered at her, sending a chill down her spine.

Tore's house sat on a corner lot in a quiet residential area outside the town center. As they parked, they admired the red brick villa, framed by a meticulously maintained garden with a sundial prominently displayed in the center of the lawn. Near the front door, a small weather station and a broom leaning casually against the wall added a touch of personality. Erik double-checked the address.

"He lived alone, right?" he asked.

"Yes, no one else is registered here," Moa replied as she pressed the doorbell.

Stepping inside, Moa's assumptions about the home were immediately upended. Instead of the cluttered space she had imagined, they found an immaculate interior. The bright and inviting decor blended Nordic minimalism with New England charm. Nautical accents were everywhere—signal flags and pennants adorned the sofa cushions, and a subtle maritime theme tied the rooms together.

"Oh," Moa said, glancing around. "This is... unexpected."

They began a quick walkthrough to understand Tore's life, and his passion for the sea became increasingly clear. A bookshelf held logbooks in a small office nook that diligently documented his seafaring career.

"He would have made an excellent forensic technician," Erik said, flipping through one of the old volumes. "He noticed details, documented everything—and look at this. He even tracked weather statistics." He gestured to a thick, leather-bound ledger on a side table by the window, accompanied by binoculars.

"I'll start dusting for fingerprints," Erik added.

While he got to work, Moa moved to the kitchen. She opened the dishwasher, hoping to find fresh DNA, but it was empty. Instead, she turned her attention to the refrigerator, where a few handwritten reminders were stuck to the door. She carefully bagged them.

Not everything matched the pristine image of the house. A foul odor wafted as she opened the trash bin, jarring against the home's otherwise spotless and tasteful appearance. Moa wrinkled her nose and noted that sometimes, the smallest inconsistencies told the most significant stories.

"No dishes, no cups this time, but hopefully, I'll find something in the trash bag."

Beneath the sink, she discovered a stash of five identical black spray paint cans from the same brand.

The black paint on his fingers?

CHAPTER TWENTY-SEVEN

MOA METHODICALLY SEARCHED the kitchen in Tore's house, sifting through the contents of the trash bag. It mostly contained food scraps, an empty toothpaste tube, and a moldy sandwich wrapped in foil. However, a discovery in one of the cabinets revealed another detail about Tore's habits: eight empty bottles of Black Label whiskey.

"What do you think a sailor's average salary is?" Moa asked, raising an eyebrow. "He has expensive taste. Black Label isn't exactly budget-friendly."

Erik paused, glancing around the now-smudged living room. The once-pristine decor was marked with dark soot from fingerprint powder.

"Well, they probably earn a decent amount," he said. "If he were at sea for weeks, it could be more than we earn. Plus, there are perks—like free meals."

Driven by the possibility of uncovering critical information, Moa turned her attention to the small desk. Her gaze fell on the open logbook once more. Beyond the weather data, she noticed cryptic phrases that resembled short diary entries. Intrigued, she carefully photographed several pages and sealed the logbook in a bag. Every detail seemed to bring them closer to understanding Tore's life—and perhaps his secrets.

"The logbook is intriguing," Moa said, glancing at Erik. "Have you found anything yet?"

Erik shook his head, adjusting his glasses. "There's a name mentioned several times—it starts with an 'S.' And there's something about someone screaming. I'll pass this to Grim; he's sharp and knows exactly what to focus on."

"Have you seen the watch collection?" Moa asked, her curiosity piqued.

Erik pointed toward a small display cabinet. "A Rolex Seamaster and a Submariner. These are incredible—and should be in a safe deposit box, not left out in the open."

"This doesn't add up," Moa said, her gaze drifting to the parking lot and the storage area behind the house. "Tore doesn't fit the profile. He's angry and drunk at his local pub, sporting a homemade tattoo. Yet he drinks extremely expensive whiskey and owns watches worth a small fortune. You'd expect high-end clothing to match, but his wardrobe consists of worn jeans and sweaters from the local supermarket."

Outside the window, a white Saab registered to Tore sat untouched in the parking lot.

"We'll have to wait and see what comes out of this afternoon's meeting," Erik replied. "Anna will be there—maybe she has some updates."

Moa turned her attention to the closets, carefully opening each door. Inside, rows of floral dresses hung neatly on hangers, and women's shoes were stored away in pristine shoeboxes. She pulled out one of the dresses, holding it up for Erik to see.

"Well, it's definitely not Tore's," Erik said with a smirk. "He was tall."

Opening the adjacent closet, Erik uncovered another surprising collection of older-style men's clothing and several uniform jackets adorned with insignias. The pieces were well-worn but hinted at a different life that deepened the mystery surrounding Tore.

"Tore's parents?" Moa asked, glancing at her watch. "We need to wrap up and come back tomorrow. Can you take some photos? I'll get started on the preliminary report."

They worked in focused silence, each absorbed in their tasks. Moa's thoughts wandered, tugged by the weight of a personal burden she preferred not to dwell on—the inevitable responsibility of managing her mother's house when the time came. Once brimming with life, the house was reduced to a collection of belongings that needed sorting, discarding, or saving.

The idea of hiring professionals to sift through someone's personal belongings was seldom discussed openly, yet it seemed an increasingly common choice. Still, it felt impersonal, almost like avoiding something deeply human. Moa remembered how stressful moving had always been, enough to trigger her itchy eczema.

The pattern was predictable: you think you don't own much, pack a few boxes, and suddenly find yourself overwhelmed. Three boxes barely contain the contents of a couple of desk drawers. It left her questioning: *What purpose did all these things serve? And how much did it all cost?*

The thought became even more bittersweet as she remembered Tomas's belongings, still carefully packed away in the basement, his entire life reduced to a few boxes from his move back to Friland. A life full of plans and promises was now paused forever.

Her phone buzzed, breaking the silence. A message flashed across the screen from an unknown number. Moa's pulse quickened as she stared at the text.

20,000 if you can manage. I'll be in touch. Be careful.

It was more than she could afford, but she couldn't turn her back on Vilda. Why couldn't Vilda get a regular job and make life simpler? As Moa wrestled with frustration, her phone buzzed with a message from Kajsa, informing her that her mother was struggling to breathe, and they were rushing her to the emergency room.

As Moa and Erik drove back to the station, the light snowfall had turned into a relentless downpour, accompanied by a biting north wind that rattled the street signs. As they passed a school, Moa's eyes caught the familiar sight of graffiti numbers scrawled across a wall.

“Stop here,” she said abruptly. “I want to check something. It’s probably a long shot, but I’d like to take a sample of that paint. It won’t hurt to have it even if it’s unrelated to our case.”

Erik didn’t need further explanation. Their instincts often aligned, making it easy to collaborate on cases without overanalyzing each other’s decisions.

“Alright,” Erik said, nodding. “We can check the graffiti at the station, too—if it hasn’t been cleaned up yet.”

“Perfect,” Moa replied, her mind already spinning with possibilities.

The haunting words from Tore’s logbook wouldn’t leave her thoughts. They echoed in her mind. Who had screamed? Had she misread it? His messy handwriting made it challenging to decipher. The contradictions in Tore’s life gnawed at her. His expensive watches were carelessly displayed in an unlocked case, his logbook left open, and his decision to leave home to meet someone, perhaps even his killer. Whoever it was, they had to be someone Tore trusted. The pieces didn’t fit, but Moa was determined to find the missing link.

CHAPTER TWENTY-EIGHT

FREDRIK STEPPED AWAY from the meeting room window, his body shivering as he swallowed two over-the-counter painkillers with a strong, bitter coffee. He winced, hoping they would dull the persistent ache in his shoulder. This was far from the fresh start he had envisioned.

A wave of nausea crept over him as he cursed the man who had shot him. That shooter probably enjoyed the comforts of a Swedish prison: two cooked meals daily, clean clothes, and counseling sessions—all funded by taxpayers. He would have access to rehabilitation programs, hearty meals, activities, and ongoing support when released. Meanwhile, Fredrik could barely get adequate pain relief, let alone focus on his job tackling the island's escalating crime.

He closed his eyes, inhaled deeply, counted to five, and exhaled slowly. Sick leave wasn't an option—not as the new guy on the job and certainly not after relocating to the islands. Even navigating Friland's welfare system had been a headache he had barely managed.

It will work out, he told himself.

* * *

The meeting room was a chaotic mix of wet coats draped over chairs. Grim had already set up his usual stack of paperwork, while Erik and Moa hurried in last, apologizing for their tardiness.

"Wasn't Anna supposed to be here?" Fredrik asked, his question punctuated by the sharp, familiar click of heels echoing down the corridor.

"Sorry I'm late," Anna said as she entered, placing an elegant, black leather portfolio on the table. The sleek design suggested it contained critical documents without the bulk of unnecessary binders. "I just released Claire. Have we started yet?"

Fredrik glanced at her and said, "We were about to begin." He turned to the noticeboard, methodically pinning up new photos and notes.

"As for Benny's murder," he continued, "we're confident that no helicopter flew over the area. The aviation authority and maritime police have both confirmed this. The evidence points to a larger boat—or possibly a ship—disposing of the car at sea."

Fredrik adjusted a few notes, pausing briefly as Moa sneezed loudly three times in rapid succession.

"Bless you," he said with a faint smile before returning his focus to the board.

Moa managed a faint smile, although the dark circles under her eyes betrayed her exhaustion.

"Anna, can you start with what you've got on Benny? Then we can move forward." Fredrik gestured toward Anna, prompting her to begin.

"We've released Claire. She's not well and seems less confident than before—likely beginning to come to terms with everything that's happened. Her hunting license has expired, and the rifle we seized was in such poor condition that she doesn't want it back. Meanwhile, our interrogator has made progress with the dockworkers in Toft, and we've received several tips worth following up."

Outside, the rain intensified, pounding against the windows. Fredrik cleared his throat and picked up a paper from his pile, and said, "As for Tore, he had no criminal record—only a few parking tickets. He inherited the house from his parents. His father was a captain on a cruise ship, primarily working in the West Indies. Tore dreamed of working there himself, but never succeeded. He was skilled at navigation and served as a captain, spending a significant portion of his career on icebreakers. More recently, he collaborated with Rune's company, which also had contracts with Jake's freight business. Tore had a steady income, but his lifestyle quickly consumed it. He occasionally gambled, drank expensive whiskey, and exhibited erratic behavior, which likely hindered his success. We've received reports about his mood swings and his involvement in minor altercations. Regarding the TikTok girl, she will remain in the hospital for a few more days for trauma counseling. Although she has provided a detailed account of her experience, it doesn't significantly contribute to our investigation." Fredrik turned his attention to Erik and Moa. "What do you have?"

Moa addressed the team, her voice steady. "You've all received the autopsy report, and now we have the ballistics report. The weapon used to kill Tore was a Sig Sauer, nine-millimeter. I've also been going through Tore's logbook, and I can't seem to let it go; it's filled with intriguing details. Grim, I know you haven't had much time, but have you found anything?"

Grim flipped through his notes. "Yes. From what I've reviewed, Tore hasn't taken any long trips in the past year. His writing style also shifts; he becomes less detailed, which may suggest fatigue, although other explanations are possible. Here are some entries that stood out: May seventeenth. Good visibility. New orders from S. Double load. Crap shift. September twenty-seventh. Double from S. Blood money. November fifteenth. Rough sea. Their screams. S. He drew a cross after the last entry. There are no crosses or doodles in any of the earlier notes."

"That's exactly what's been nagging at me," Moa said, wiping her nose. "Who screamed? And who is 'S?'"

* * *

Fredrik lingered in the staff room, sensing Moa's subtle distance and noticing the coolness in her demeanor.

"Are you coming down with something?" he asked hesitantly, wincing at how awkward it sounded as she blew her nose.

"Not exactly," Moa replied. "I got chilled out there in the rain. I'll be fine—I'm off tomorrow and plan to rest. We can talk later. Or are you seeing Ingrid again?"

Fredrik caught the edge in her tone; a flicker of jealousy was unmistakable.

"I'm bringing home some paperwork," he stated. "It'll just be me, a takeout, and a stack of reports. My shoulder is acting up again, so I need some downtime." He touched his shoulder to emphasize his point and briefly explained Dr. Ulrik's recent advice.

Moa's expression softened, and the jealousy in her tone started to fade. "That's tough. The authorities might have reviewed him. A lot of doctors have come under scrutiny lately for prescribing strong medications to the wrong patients. Regulations have really tightened. Is it as bad as last year?"

"Unfortunately, yes. I'm trying not to panic, but it's hard—I still have to keep going."

Moa placed a reassuring hand on his back. "I'll ask Dr. Alicia if she can help. She's Mom's doctor and specializes in geriatrics, so she might know what to do."

"Dr. Alicia?" Fredrik asked, a flicker of curiosity crossing his face.

"She's great," Moa said, laughing lightly. "Don't let her geriatric specialty fool you."

Fredrik chuckled softly, and the tension between them began to ease, warming the moment enough to leave things on a better note.

CHAPTER TWENTY-NINE

MOA DROPPED THE BAG of new clothes in Tomas's small apartment, her movements abrupt and unsteady. She paused to catch her breath.

For heaven's sake, relax.

The day was slipping away faster than she wished for. Despite the whole day off, her to-do list felt endless—errands, tasks, and a trip to the hairdresser to wash her wig.

Tomas's eyes were bloodshot, a clear sign he'd been crying. The weight of everything he'd lost loomed heavy in the room, a pain too profound to be mended by a handful of therapy sessions. Moa knew better than to offer hollow platitudes about how things could be worse or improve with time. Tomas had every right to grieve for as long as he needed. His dreams lay in ruins—years of studying felt wasted, crushing loans weighed on him, his research career had vanished, and the prospect of starting a family seemed distant, if not impossible.

"I stopped to see Mom on my way here," Moa said softly. "She was admitted last night, but she's not in immediate danger. They're keeping her for observation today. Kajsa's with her."

Tomas nodded, his face unreadable. He'd quickly adapted to reading lips, something Moa was still trying to master. Together, they'd even created their rudimentary sign language—a small victory in their effort to feel like life was moving forward, no matter how slow the progress. But their conversations always seemed to circle back to illness, loss, and medication. It was draining, and Moa longed for a change.

She began unpacking the clothes she'd brought, showing him each piece. They were neatly washed and ironed, and as usual, she'd gone overboard with the fabric softener. The scent of crisp freshness filled the room, a temporary reprieve from the suffocating weight of reality.

Tomas ran his hand over the soft fabric of the pajamas. Lifting the garment to his nose, he inhaled deeply, letting the fresh scent bring a flicker of comfort to his tired eyes. Using a combination of their improvised sign language, shared gestures, and the few words he could manage, Tomas conveyed that he was doing okay.

Moa considered telling him about Fredrik, but decided it wasn't the right time.

Tomas's apartment at the rehabilitation facility was temporary. The plan was to move him to a handicap-accessible apartment once his strength improved. While the doctors made no guarantees, they remained cautiously optimistic that Tomas might be able to walk short distances. Chronic pain, however, remained a possibility.

Moa had already begun scouting apartments in Toft, researching subsidies they might qualify for. The municipality, predictably, was resistant, urging them to accept one of the already-available adapted apartments. Budget cuts were always the excuse, and Moa knew they were reluctant to allocate additional funds. But she refused to tell Tomas, unwilling to let him face the disappointment just yet. She was determined he wouldn't be stuck in a shabby, pre-furnished apartment with no decent view, no matter what it took.

Her gaze lingered on the scars that traced his face, the evidence of his struggle etched into his skin. She wished she could take his pain and frustration away, even momentarily.

"Read to me," Tomas signed.

Moa noticed her shoulders were hunched so tightly they nearly touched her ears. She forced herself to relax with a deep breath, letting the tension drain from her body. This was the only place she needed to be—with her brother. She focused on the moment, willing herself to be present.

They sat together by the window, silently watching life unfold outside. Moa wanted to bring Tomas out into the world, but the thought of wrestling with jackets, scarves, gloves, and hats felt overwhelming. Life seemed like an endless postponement, always waiting for a "later" that never came.

Her gaze landed on the travel magazine resting atop the pile of books on the kitchen table. She picked it up and flipped through the glossy pages, filled with images of must-see destinations: narrow alleys unsuitable for a wheelchair, uneven cobblestone streets, and vibrant, oversized headlines promoting the "Top 5 Destinations of the Year." The centerfold showcased an article on luxury cruises through the Greek islands—a trip where disembarking from the boat was optional.

Moa's mind wandered to their mother, who had once dreamed of island-hopping through Greece as a teenager. She had fantasized about moving there, opening a small restaurant, and living each day in the moment. It was a whimsical, secret dream she carried until illness forced her to share it. One evening, she confessed to Moa, saying she had always imagined taking them to the Greek islands one day. She would talk for hours about her dream, poring over maps and showing them photos of the idyllic islands. Her dad was a restless soul, working his way across the North Sea aboard various oil rigs. Moa's mom grew tired of his empty promises shortly after Tomas was born. From then on, her dad became more of a dream than a presence in Moa's life—a longing for him to be there, sit in the audience at her school play, and be part of the family vacations other kids excitedly planned. But he was never there. Instead, Moa learned to lie to her friends. Sometimes, he would show up unexpectedly, arms full of lavish gifts, only to vanish again for months. He had not even returned her last call. So, time slipped away. With little money for trips and the demands of being a single mother, the dream remained just that—a dream. Before they knew it, Moa and Tomas had grown into adults. The idea of fulfilling that dream felt as distant as the islands themselves.

Moa pointed out the ship, the islands, the quaint villages, and the swaying palm trees in the photos. "We could disembark, take a taxi around the island, return to the ship, or sit at a café in the port," she said. "It doesn't have to be complicated."

Tomas smiled faintly, leaning forward before wincing—a grimace hinting at his pain. It was time for his afternoon medication.

As Moa continued reading the article about the cruise, a determination grew within her. They would visit the Greek islands within the year. They'd fly first class, stay in a luxurious suite, and if necessary, she'd hire an assistant to come along. It would cost a fortune, but for once, her visit with Tomas left her feeling stronger instead of drained.

Dr. Alicia, who was treating their mother, had mentioned that stress likely contributed to the rapid progression of her illness. Moa's mother had a terminal diagnosis and was expected to pass away by spring, possibly even sooner. For Moa and Tomas, ALS loomed like a dark cloud over their future.

Moa refused to dwell on the thought that Tomas's suffering could worsen if he, too, developed the disease. Would she die before him? She prayed fervently that he would never be left alone. There were too many unknowns—perhaps they would both succumb to it, or maybe neither would.

But for now, they needed to focus on the present and make the most of the time they had left together.

CHAPTER THIRTY

SALON CUTTING CREW had recently relocated from Nordby, much to Moa's relief—no more long journeys to get her wig sorted. The salon's owner, Nora, represented comfort and familiarity, having been the family's trusted hairdresser during their summer vacations in Nordby. Moa had remained loyal to Nora, drawn to her warmth and the salon's retro charm. Despite decades passing, Nora had kept the original eighties decor, insisting that the cheerful pastels of that era never went out of style.

"How are you?" Nora asked, tilting her head with a familiar gentleness.

The room was filled with the unmistakable scent of Chanel No. 5, Nora's signature fragrance.

"I'm good, thanks," Moa replied, managing a faint smile. "Taking things bit by bit. Fredrik's back on the island."

"I can tell," Nora said with a gentle smile. "You're glowing."

Nora carefully removed Moa's wig and slipped on her reading glasses, which always hung from a delicate chain around her neck. She examined the wig's interior with her practiced hands.

"I was out at sea again," Moa explained. "I rinsed the wig when I returned, but you always make it look better. We had to recover a body. The dry suit hood offers some protection for the wig, but it still needs a proper wash. Honestly, I've been thinking about giving it up entirely, but I don't want to draw attention. And the wig was so expensive—it feels like a waste."

"I understand," Nora said softly. "If you want, I can show you some simple styles to give you more variety. How does that sound?"

Moa met Nora's calm, reassuring gaze in the mirror. Tears welled in her eyes, threatening to spill over as the weight of everything she was carrying settled between them.

"Oh, dear, is it your mom? I didn't want to pry," Nora said gently.

Before Moa could respond, the door opened, and Nora set the wig down carefully. She handed Moa a folded copy of the Times of Friland before turning to assist a customer.

Moa's gaze fell on the front page, where a vibrant photo of lawyer Jake Lund dominated the layout. The headline announced his nomination for Entrepreneur of the Year, with the ceremony scheduled for the Ostara

Carnival in the spring. The article lauded Jake's remarkable commitment to environmental initiatives, particularly his charitable program, Tires of Hope, in Senegal. The project created jobs, offered education to children, and recycled thousands of tires that might have otherwise polluted the environment, serving as an inspiring example of sustainable entrepreneurship.

Below the feature on Jake, a smaller article caught her attention. It was a brief notice of photographer Benny Palm's passing, describing him as a diligent and talented creative whose work had left a lasting impression.

Nora returned and said, "Now, where were we? Let's start with the usual scalp treatment. I've got some new products, nothing miraculous, but they smell divine. I'll send you home with a starter kit to try out."

Her warm, familiar voice grounded Moa, providing a slight reprieve from the chaos outside the salon doors.

The words were a soothing balm for Moa's weary soul. Nora's salon was one of the few places where she could truly relax, a space that felt like stepping back into carefree childhood days, leaving stress at the door and letting herself believe in comforting words because they were genuine and heartfelt. For a brief moment, she could let go of the relentless search for answers to life's darkest questions and the unyielding pressure of meticulously documenting every critical detail of a crime scene.

"It's just… There's so much going on," Moa admitted, her voice wavering. "Mom keeps going back and forth to the emergency room. One moment, it feels like it's the end, then she recovers a bit. And the next thing I know, the equipment fails. On top of that, there's Tomas—there's always the responsibility for him."

Nora handed her a box of tissues and carefully washed Moa's scalp, creating a gentle lather. Tiny strands of hair were beginning to grow at the nape of Moa's neck, and she silently prayed for a miracle.

"If it ever becomes overwhelming, you know you're always welcome here," Nora said softly, her tone infused with reassurance.

"Thank you," Moa murmured, closing her eyes. She allowed herself to push aside her worries for a moment, focusing on the brighter aspects of her life. She envisioned the Greek islands and made a mental note to ask Fredrik if he'd like to join her on the trip.

Nora's voice brought her back. "It's so sad about Benny. He used to come in for haircuts occasionally. It seemed like he had a lot going on. He had even met a girl up in Breda."

Moa's peaceful thoughts vanished instantly, yanking her back into the sharp reality of work. She leaned forward, her expression shifting to one of intense focus.

"When did that happen? What else do you know?"

Nora dried her hands and grabbed her calendar, flipping through the pages where her appointments were noted in pencil.

"He was reported missing on April third," Moa said, carefully omitting the crucial detail that Benny had last been seen arriving in Breda on February twenty-fifth. That piece of information was something she needed to keep to herself for now.

"Yes, I remember—it was right around the twentieth," Nora said, pausing to think. "I'd had a plumber here earlier in the month, and the salon still wasn't fully set up. Benny was actually my very first customer, so he stands out in my memory. I had opened just before Christmas, and he came in three times.

"The last time he was here was on February twenty-third. That day, he mentioned that he'd met a girl and was in a hurry. Luckily for him, I didn't have many bookings that day, so he had time to spruce up. He wanted to look his best for her. She was a photographer, and they had planned to combine their date with a photo shoot.

"He mentioned something about the limestone quarry in Breda, the new architect-designed office they built there a few years ago. I remember how cheerful he was, almost like an excited kid."

Moa's pulse raced as adrenaline surged through her. She seized her phone and rapidly messaged Fredrik.

Come to the salon, Cutting Crew, ASAP. Important lead.

Noticing Moa's intensity, Nora hesitated, guilt flashing across her face. "I should have thought to inform the police about this sooner," she said quietly.

Moa placed a reassuring hand on her arm. "Don't worry—often, the smallest and most unexpected details help solve a case. And this? This could be the piece we need to tie everything together."

Nora nodded, clearly relieved, as Moa's keen mind raced, making connections and getting ready for the next step.

* * *

When Moa turned off toward Odde, the sky was pitch black. Nora's comforting words still echoed in her mind—her assurance that Moa's hair would grow back by summer had provided some solace. Moa carried a luxurious set of hair care products in the passenger seat, knowing she would have the house to herself while her mother remained in the hospital.

The peace was shattered when headlights suddenly appeared in her rearview mirror. A car approached rapidly, its high beams glaring directly into her eyes. The driver started flashing the lights and honking aggressively, quickly closing the gap between them.

Moa gripped the wheel tightly, her pulse quickening as she slowed on the narrow road, hugging the edge to allow the other car to pass. However, instead of overtaking, the vehicle remained dangerously close, tailgating her every move.

She took a deep breath and pressed the gas pedal on a straight stretch, attempting to create some distance. The tension snapped when she heard a metallic scrape—the other car had brushed against hers. Moa adjusted her rearview mirror to shield her from the blinding lights, her hands trembling.

Up ahead, she noticed the turnoff to the soccer field a few hundred meters beyond a curve. Bracing herself, she pressed her neck against the headrest and accelerated. The car behind honked wildly and swerved to the side, as if trying to force her off the road.

Despite the streetlights, Moa could only discern the vague outline of a figure in the other car, their face partially obscured. The vehicle—a black Skoda—lurched aggressively toward her. With her heart pounding, she made a split-second decision and turned sharply into the soccer field parking lot, her tires crunching over gravel as she sought safety.

She slammed on the brakes, causing the car to fishtail wildly in the loose gravel before finally coming to a stop. Her heart raced as she watched the Skoda screech to a halt, narrowly avoiding oncoming traffic. Her mouth felt parched, adrenaline coursing through her veins as she gripped the wheel and eased her car back onto the road. Spotting a vehicle heading toward Toft, she fell behind it, maintaining a safe distance, her pulse still pounding in her ears.

CHAPTER THIRTY-ONE

FREDRIK FELT GRATEFUL for having a short walk to work instead of being stuck in traffic. The relentless rain had finally ceased, but the sudden drop in temperature had turned the wet roads into hazardous ice rinks. A thin layer of snow had covered the ice overnight, resulting in the emergency room being inundated with cases of broken bones.

A week had passed since their attempt to decipher the cryptic entries in Tore's logbook, and the investigation into Benny's murder remained frustratingly stagnant. Hoping for a lead, Fredrik went directly to Nora, the hairdresser, to gather any information she had about Benny's supposed date.

Back at the station, Fredrik nearly collided with Grim in the corridor, who was precariously balancing a steaming cup of coffee on top of a stack of folders.

“Any updates from your friend about the stalker?” Grim asked, raising an eyebrow as he adjusted the folders.

“He blocked the number. Did you discover anything new about the woman Benny was supposed to meet from the dating site?” Fredrik asked.

“Come into my office for a moment. I have some new information to share, and we might as well discuss it now,” Grim replied.

Grim’s office could easily be mistaken for a library. Every inch of the walls was lined with shelves filled with textbooks. He had once mentioned that he retained information better from paper books—digital versions didn’t have the same effect. Fredrik had to admit it was likely true.

“Here’s what I have so far,” Grim said, swiveling his monitor to face Fredrik.

He opened a report on the screen. “I found some chat history on one of Benny’s devices, including screenshots of messages. After piecing it together, here’s what we know: the woman Benny was supposed to meet was a lure—a fake profile. She claimed to own a Breda clothing store and expressed a passion for photography. Benny, meanwhile, exaggerated his lifestyle, discussing frequent photo trips to New York and entering contests.”

“The dating site isn’t cooperating,” Grim continued, frustration lacing his voice. “They claim they’re not responsible for members’ behavior and don’t store deleted profiles. Digging further will take time. On top of that, the fake profile was well-protected—it used a VPN and left almost no digital trace."

Fredrik leaned in, his mind racing with implications. A well-constructed fake profile and a carefully laid trap—this case was growing darker with each new lead.

Fredrik suppressed the urge to scream in frustration. Every time it seemed like he was making progress, something pulled the rug out from under him. He forced himself to sit down, took a steadying breath, and concentrated on Grim's calm, methodical voice.

"I've uncovered a small pattern," Grim began, his tone measured. "Rune has been paying Tore for what he calls 'services.' On its own, that's not unusual. But here's where it gets interesting: around the same time as these transactions, Rune's yacht was spotted in the same area, according to the maritime police. A couple of cargo ships were also seen on nearby routes."

Grim leaned forward, pulling up more data on his screen. "I checked Rune's website. His company doesn't offer pre-set tours. Instead, customers rent the boats with a crew and chart their own routes. But here's the thing—there's nothing noteworthy in those waters, especially in the middle of the North Sea during winter—no whales, no seals, nothing that would attract tourists."

"Fishing? Maybe. But in the middle of the night? Unlikely." Grim paused, narrowing his eyes at the screen. "I'll need to consult someone familiar with the area to confirm. For now, I've documented my findings and flagged some questions. Anna's eager to bring Rune in for questioning, but I'd prefer to keep him under observation a bit longer."

Fredrik agreed, the pieces starting to shift in his mind. This was not a straightforward case; every small clue appeared to lead to a larger, murkier puzzle.

"We need more than just Rune's boat being out at sea," Fredrik said, straightening his back. "I'll talk to Anna about arranging a wiretap. So far, Rune has been cooperative, and there's nothing unusual on the surface. Jake called me almost immediately after the news of Tore's death broke. He spoke highly of the times he hired Tore through Rune."

Fredrik paused, his expression clouding slightly. "But here's the odd part—Erik and Moa discovered a match in the graffiti spreading throughout the town. The paint cans beneath Tore's sink matched the color of his fingers, fingertips, and the walls."

"Good work," Grim said. "But why would a middle-aged man spray paint graffiti on walls?"

Fredrik shrugged, frustrated by the inexplicable quirks of human behavior. Tore's few remaining relatives had shown little interest in his death. They had fallen out long ago over their parents' inheritance, a sad yet all-too-common story.

Rubbing his shoulder, Fredrik contemplated Dr. Alicia's words. She had been blunt: he needed to stop straining it unnecessarily and seriously consider changing his duties or dictating his reports. Her prognosis had been grim but truthful. Fredrik wasn't ready to involve occupational health services yet—they were notorious for dragging out investigations and often assigned officers to mind-numbing tasks, like sorting paperwork in archives. That was a fate Fredrik wasn't willing to accept.

For now, he had enough painkillers to last through the next three weeks. By then, he hoped to have found a solution or perhaps, against all odds, to be cured by a miracle.

* * *

Fredrik's phone had been blissfully silent since he blocked the number sending him taunting messages. However, only a few hours had passed, and he had been naive to think it would end so easily. His screen lit up again.

"You can't get rid of me. There are rumors about you. You know the truth, don't you? Fancy a pizza tonight?"

A notification popped up from the booking site: a new guest review had been posted for his cottage. Fredrik had lost track of who was staying there since he relied on a rental management company to handle the details. A few reviews seemed to have slipped through the cracks amid the flood of recent messages.

The headline immediately captured his attention: complaints about mold and inadequate cleaning. He skimmed through the text, cluttered with spelling and grammatical errors. This wasn't the first review of its kind. Over the past week, a few similar posts had emerged, alleging that the walls were covered in mold and hinting at sinister rumors about a body being found on a neighboring property.

He had addressed the mold issue caused by water damage months ago, and the "body" was a set of bone fragments connected to a missing person. None of this was relevant now.

CHAPTER THIRTY-TWO

MOA COULDN'T DETERMINE if she had truly slept or simply dreamed that she had. The gun beneath her pillow provided a small but reassuring sense of protection, while having Erik by her side at The Vault added another layer of security. She had skipped breakfast without feeling hungry, and even now, she found it difficult to eat lunch.

After shaking off the tailgater the night before, she drove straight to the station. There, she handed over the dashcam footage and filed a detailed report. She didn't mention the warning from Vilda—it was a personal matter, not something she was ready to share yet. Later, she planned to transfer the money Vilda had requested. Their fragile connection had been forged through years of pulling each other out of tight spots, but it was becoming increasingly tangled and harder to break. Sometimes, Moa reflected, the only option was to take control and handle things yourself—no matter how complicated it became.

"Have you told anyone what happened?" Erik asked, scraping the last bit of sauce from his plate.

Moa shook her head. "I haven't had the chance—or the energy. I don't want to worry anyone. It all happened so fast, but it rattled me. I keep telling myself it was just some drunk idiot who watched too many action movies and decided to mess with me at random. By the way, your new glasses look great."

"Thanks," Erik said with a small smile as he adjusted them. "I needed stronger lenses, and they've made a huge difference. My headaches are completely gone."

"You see how even a small change can have a big impact," Fredrik said as he approached their table with a tray.

Setting it down, he turned to Moa. "By the way, have you been in an accident? I noticed a dent in your car."

"It's just a minor dent—not worth repairing. The deductible will cost more than the repair itself."

She hadn't lied, but she didn't elaborate either. If Fredrik had asked directly whether someone had tailgated her last night, she might have admitted it. However, now wasn't the time to address that drama.

"So," Erik said, redirecting the conversation, "did your vacation plans work out, Fredrik? Did you get the weeks you wanted?"

Fredrik poured himself a glass of milk and took a deliberate bite of a cinnamon bun. "Unfortunately, no," Fredrik said, shaking his head. "I saw the announcement on the intranet about summer vacations. We will need more staff than usual because of the summer festival. I think they've managed it pretty well, though. Back on the mainland, the last minute was always a chaotic scramble. You'd think summer was a surprise that popped up suddenly every year, and we were perpetually short-staffed."

He leaned forward slightly and said, "There are going to be seven stages at Vallarna Beach, and they're running free buses to and from Toft to help spread out the visitors. They're even setting up a beer tent in the old port, so extra staff will definitely be needed. Oh, and get this: they've got a punk band from Finland, another from the mainland, and—wait for it—a boy band from Japan."

Moa erupted in laughter. "Oh my God! I regret my decision to sign up for patrol during the festival. But at least the pay is decent."

She glanced at Fredrik with a playful grin. Fredrik continued, "Dennis has already booked the flight—a smart move since prices are ridiculous. He'll stay at the cottage up in Nordby, not minding the distance. I might stay a couple of nights myself, but let's be honest, I'll have to pretend I'm on vacation."

Erik stood, collecting his cutlery and placing Moa's plate and utensils onto his tray before carrying them to the dish rack.

"We're planning a trip this fall," Moa told Fredrik, her tone casual yet inviting. "How about joining Tomas and me in Greece this September?"

Fredrik looked up, caught off guard, with a faint milk streak on his upper lip.

"I never thought you would ask," he said, surprise and curiosity mixing in his voice.

* * *

A small stack of papers sat on Moa's desk, waiting for her attention. Instead, she curled up in the visitor's chair and opened Google Maps. She wanted to explore its features and compile a list of places to visit, aiming for a clear overview. Stockholm was one of the cities she wanted to explore further, so she added it to her list.

As she worked, she heard laughter and the distinct click of high heels in the corridor, guessing that Anna was nearby. Moa's fingers glided slowly across the screen, navigating toward the Greek islands. There were countless options to choose from. She selected Kea, recalling her mother's description of the island's famous landmark, the smiling lion, and saved the location. Then, she turned her attention to Friland, casually browsing among the islands and imagining a long weekend getaway with Fredrik.

As Moa absentmindedly swiped across her screen, she accidentally pinned a spot in the sea off Toft. A small box popped up, displaying the location's coordinates. Her heart skipped a beat, and the fatigue vanished instantly. The fifteen-digit number looked eerily familiar.

Frowning, she opened her photos and scrolled quickly to the image of the graffiti that Tore had painted. *Coordinates? Could it really be that simple?*

She quickly typed the number into the search box, and the pin dropped onto a location in the sea southeast of Friland. Moa saved the spot and immediately pulled up the report from Benny's apartment. Her hands shook slightly as she scanned the pages. The numbers scrawled on the back of the instruction manual matched the coordinates Tore had painted on the walls in Toft.

Moa glanced up, adrenaline coursing through her veins, as Anna arrived at her office door, her expression shifting to surprise just as she was about to knock.

"Coordinates," Moa blurted out, her voice sharp with urgency. "It's coordinates! I need to call Fredrik."

Before she could reach for her phone, it rang. Dr. Alicia's name flashed on the screen. Her heart pounded as she hesitated, torn between ignoring the call and sharing her discovery with Anna. Ultimately, she chose to answer, bracing herself.

"Your mother is in the hospital," Dr. Alicia said solemnly. "She grabbed a sharp object and attempted to take her own life."

Moa's stomach dropped as the weight of the revelation crashed into her racing thoughts.

CHAPTER THIRTY-THREE

FREDRIK CURSED AS the doorbell rang. He had spilled an entire cup of tea on his pants in his haste to get ready. Having barely managed to dash home to change, he was now pulling on a clean pair of jeans when the bell echoed again.

He opened and found a courier holding a neatly wrapped box, white paper tied with black silk ribbons. Fredrik stared at it, wrestling with whether to open it. Blocking the harassing number had been a futile attempt to stop the madness. The deliveries kept coming, and the stalker's messages had only escalated. Changing his number felt pointless; the stalker already knew his address.

Fredrik's fear had curdled into a volatile mixture of anger and indifference. Against his better judgment, he opened the box.

Inside were two urns—this time for humans. One bore his name; the other, Moa's.

"Holy shit!"

This was no longer harassment; it had crossed a line. Fredrik's jaw tightened as he stuffed the delivery note and the restaurant's address for the pizzas into his pocket. He would handle it as soon as he returned to the station.

As he entered the stairwell, he almost bumped into Ingrid, who was carrying two grocery bags.

"Let me help you," he offered, taking one. "One arm is still functioning well—for now."

"Are you in pain?" she asked, her voice softening.

"Yes, my left shoulder. I need to get back to work. See you later—and take care."

Fredrik stepped outside, carefully navigating the slippery sidewalk as he dodged piles of snow. The salt spread to melt the ice had done its job, but it left a gritty, slushy mess mixed with the sand to prevent slipping. He couldn't help but think about how much he preferred the untouched beauty of fresh snow, even if its charm never lasted long.

As he arrived at the station, Moa called.

"Fredrik," she said, her voice tinged with urgency. He could tell immediately that they had uncovered something crucial.

After a brief conversation, Fredrik forwarded the new information to the marine police. They would investigate the coordinates in the area and report back to him as soon as possible. A glimmer of hope sparked; perhaps they were finally closing in on answers.

When Fredrik picked up his access cards as a new employee, he never imagined he would have any reason to return to the personnel department. Yet now, the HR manager was waiting for him. The urgent message demanded that he come immediately, and no explanation was given.

He entered a room that could only be described as a beige overload. A slender man dressed in beige sat against a beige wall backdrop, with a painting of a brown autumn scene hanging on the wall. The air was oppressively dry, with the radiators cranked too high. The man muttered something while gesturing toward the visitor's chair.

"We've received a complaint regarding you," he began, his voice flat. "It's anonymous, as these things often are, but we must investigate. This will, of course, take some time. I have a few questions for you."

Adrenaline surged through Fredrik's veins, and his stomach tightened. He stiffened in his seat, instinctively straightening his back. The beige room appeared to close in on him, the details blurring as a chill crept into the space between him and the man sifting through a pile of papers.

The man pulled out an A4 sheet, and Fredrik caught a glimpse of the details—marital status, address, CV, and age—neatly typed at the top.

"We need to investigate everything thoroughly, which, as I mentioned, will take time," the man repeated, his tone nearly mechanical.

"Okay." He kept his voice steady, although every nerve in his body screamed for answers. He waited, confident the beige man would finally reveal the complaint.

"You're new to the island, right?"

"Yes," Fredrik responded, his tone sharp.

"I hope you don't mind my bluntness, but do you have any conflicts with anyone? Any enemies? Someone who might seek revenge?"

The question lingered in the dry, overheated air like a challenge, causing Fredrik's pulse to quicken. Whoever filed the complaint wasn't trying to stir up trouble—they wanted to bring him down.

Before Fredrik could respond, the man pressed on, his tone measured yet heavy. "The best approach here is honesty. According to the complainant, you've made unwanted physical advances. They are considering filing a rape charge. The complainant also claims several women are prepared to testify against you."

The words struck Fredrik like a physical blow. The stress from the stalker, the horrifying discovery of the urns bearing his and Moa's names, and the creeping guilt of not reporting the situation sooner all came crashing down on him. His silence, though born of caution, now seemed a double-edged sword, leaving him vulnerable to having his actions twisted against him.

It had gone too far. He needed to take control of the situation, but doubts clouded his mind. Could he even trust his colleagues? What if someone at the station was involved and plotting to frame him? What if they tampered with the investigation into his stalker? The spiraling thoughts only tightened the noose of anxiety around him.

Fredrik's mind drifted to Moa. He needed to tell her about the urn with her name on it. But how? He didn't want to burden or complicate the little time she had left with her mother. He decided to ask if she had received any threats or accusations to test the waters before involving her in a broader investigation.

"I need to share something with you," he said to the beige man, his voice tense. "But I need time to write everything down properly. May I get back to you?"

To his surprise, the beige man said, "Of course. Just don't take too long."

Fredrik left the office quickly, his legs trembling. When he reached his desk, the shoulder pain he had suppressed for hours returned with a vengeance. Cold sweat prickled his skin, and his chest felt tight. He clenched his fists to fight off the tears threatening to spill and swallowed hard to suppress the urge to vomit.

"Shit."

His phone rang, jolting him from his spiraling thoughts. A woman from the marine police, her voice rough and hoarse, was on the line. Fredrik held his breath, desperate for good news, something concrete and rational to cut through the chaos.

"We've identified the coordinates," the woman said. "The site is a deep-sea trench descending at least five hundred meters. We're deploying sonar for further exploration. I'll update you as soon as we discover anything significant."

CHAPTER THIRTY-FOUR

CAPITANOS PREFERRED TO use his weapon—a clean, efficient, and bloodless way to finish the job. It suited the new chapter of his life: one he found strangely exhilarating, though physically demanding. However, this wasn't something he intended to make a habit of.

The man before him cowered, raising his shaking hands in a futile attempt to shield his face, his voice breaking into frantic shouts.

So damned *unnecessary*.

The room pulsed with adrenaline. For Capitanos, this was an intoxicating rush of power, a reminder of his dominance. For his victim, it represented raw terror, a suffocating dread of impending death.

"You're taking unnecessary risks," Capitanos growled, his voice calm but venomous. "You're such a bloody fool."

He hadn't expected a coherent answer—he didn't need one. The words filled the silence, a void he could not endure.

The small, soundproof office was perfect. Naturally, it had been his idea; every good idea was his. Then, someone mediocre came along, copied it, and basked in the acclaim. He was done with that nonsense. Lady Luck chose her winners and losers, and the man kneeling before him was undeniably in the latter camp—a pathetic nobody playing a role he could never truly own.

The baton swung down again, harder this time. The dull thud of the blows echoed in the room, each strike louder than the last. Then, silence: eerie and absolute.

Capitanos finished the job by spraying slogans on the walls, his movements precise and deliberate. He paused, carefully peeling off his gloves. Closing his eyes, he relaxed and focused on his breathing, steadying himself.

As if nothing had happened, he left the building and slid into the driver's seat. Starting the car, he let a faint smile touch his lips. *Just another ordinary day at the office*, he thought, the engine purring as he drove off into the night.

CHAPTER THIRTY-FIVE

DR. ALICIA'S WORDS about the mother's suicide attempt echoed relentlessly in Moa's mind, overshadowing what should have been a pleasant lunch. Although she managed to engage in the conversation at the table, her thoughts drifted far away, focused on her mother. The timing of Alicia's call couldn't have been worse; there was no opportunity to leave and visit until later that evening.

"I'm going to die anyway; what difference does it make?" her mother had said, the words slicing deeper than any wound.

According to the medical staff, Vera had somehow obtained a sharp object and attempted to cut her wrists. Fortunately, her weakened grip prevented the injuries from being life-threatening, but the emotional toll was far more severe.

Moa couldn't shake her frustration, wishing Dr. Alicia—or even Kajsa—had noticed some warning signs of her mother's despair. Yet deep down, Moa knew that blaming others wouldn't change anything. No matter how hard she tried to shift the guilt, it always circled back to her.

And what could anyone say to her mother now? Platitudes about bravery in the face of death? Hollow reassurances that everything would be fine when it clearly wasn't? Moa's chest tightened, her helplessness suffocating her as she searched in vain for answers she didn't possess.

Moa took a deep breath, finding a small measure of comfort in knowing her mother had been given tranquilizers and would sleep through the night. It wasn't the ideal solution, but it offered a brief reprieve for now. Without hesitation, she quickly sent a message to Kajsa, asking her to call Dr. Alicia. There was no time for lengthy personal conversations—Kajsa was competent, well-paid, and fully equipped to handle the situation. Moa had to trust her.

* * *

Moa transferred the money to Vilda, although this time, doubt lingered about whether she would ever see it returned. Furthermore, Tomas's rehabilitation facility manager had conveniently sent an invoice for what she termed "additional expenses." Lacking the time or energy to sift through the fine print, Moa paid it without hesitation. The details were buried in a tiny print PDF, clearly designed to dissuade overwhelmed individuals from contesting it. A clever way to save time for everyone involved—except, of course, for the one footing the bill.

In an ideal world, Moa envisioned Tomas living in his own apartment within a shared building where she could also stay. With an assistant to help him and daily activities to connect him with others, he would receive the best rehabilitation while maintaining a sense of independence. She even considered options abroad but hesitated to send him away alone. Deep down, she acknowledged the truth: his injuries were permanent. The goal wasn't to reverse them but to create a sustainable, secure daily life where Tomas could thrive with the right balance of support and freedom.

Erik's voice snapped her back to reality. "We're still waiting for a match on the tire tracks near the lighthouse," he said, his tone detached, as if he were speaking more to himself than to her.

"Something will come up," Moa replied, refocusing. "According to the marine police, the coordinates indicate a deep depression in the sea—several hundred meters."

Erik furrowed his brow. "I'm not following."

"Fredrik called," she clarified. "The marine police are using sonar to investigate the site. Can you cover for me for an hour? I need to stop by the hospital. It's Mom."

"No problem. Just stay focused on the job," Erik said, his voice steady yet laced with concern. "You know how easily mistakes can happen when you're tired."

Moa picked up on the subtle tension in his words. "Is there something specific on your mind? We need to be honest with each other."

Erik hesitated before speaking. "Only a couple of small things. You put the wrong date on some evidence bags at the cliff. I know you weren't yourself that night, but I covered for you."

"That place probably affects me more than I realize," Moa admitted. "I can't stop thinking about all the suicides that have occurred there. I need to get a grip on myself."

She paused, gathering her thoughts and shedding the self-reproach that weighed her down. Erik had her back—a rarity in their field, where colleagues and management could easily turn against you if you made a mistake.

Moa silently thanked him and resolved to gather herself. The days ahead would be turbulent, and she would need every ounce of focus to navigate what was coming.

CHAPTER THIRTY-SIX

FREDRIK WAITED PATIENTLY at The Norse Inn, his attention drawn to the sound of the mistletoe bell as Moa entered. The familiar chime stirred the usually alert dog, though it took a few seconds before its bark joined in. Fredrik had grown accustomed to the noise, even finding comfort in the reminder of time passing.

Standing up, he hung Moa's jacket over the back of a chair. Her exhaustion was evident on her face.

"I could see Mom at the hospital for a bit," she said softly.

Fredrik stayed silent, sensing the weight of her words.

"She attempted to take her own life," Moa continued. "They'll keep her for a night or two. At times, I wish she could pass away peacefully. Does that sound awful?"

Fredrik remained still. There were no words—nothing anyone could say to make it better.

Hanna stepped in, her cheerful presence cutting through the heaviness. "I've baked a blueberry pie if you're interested. I picked the berries last summer."

"Oh, yum!" Moa replied, managing a slight smile. "With whipped cream?"

Hanna gently placed her hand on Moa's shoulder. "You'll each receive a bowl of cream—enjoy as much as you like," she said before disappearing into the kitchen.

"She's worth her weight in gold," Fredrik said, breaking the silence. "This place feels like a spa for the soul after work. Even Ingrid seems more reasonable these days. I can actually hold a conversation with her now."

Moa's expression changed, a flicker of displeasure crossing her face.

A British couple in windbreakers entered. Hanna's face lit up as she greeted them, kissing them on the cheeks. Their lively conversation made it clear they were regular visitors. The room felt lighter for a moment as the tension eased into the background.

"We had to take a detour. There's trouble at the port," the man announced loudly as he slid into his seat.

"Yes, it's dreadful. Truly dreadful," the woman huffed, taking a menu. "I don't know what's happened to this world. And here in Toft—it was once so peaceful."

"It seems to be climate activists," the man continued. "They do this regularly back in the UK as well."

"That's right," Hanna chimed in. "This protest was planned and is usually peaceful. They aim to make their presence known."

At their table, Fredrik quietly swapped plates with Moa, giving her the larger slice of pie. He sensed she wasn't eating well, probably surviving on protein shakes and nuts. But now wasn't the time for a lecture.

Ingrid leaned in, whispering softly to Fredrik. "Some pizzas have arrived. I told the delivery guy to leave them on the floor."

Her sweet perfume lingered in the air. Moa frowned in confusion, her eyes following Ingrid as she disappeared behind the bar. Fredrik knew it was time to be honest. He needed to tell Moa about the stalker, the pizzas, and the urns. Each time they met privately, work and the latest case dominated their conversations, leaving little room for personal matters.

"For heaven's sake, why didn't you tell me sooner?" Moa exclaimed as he finally started to explain. "You need to report this."

"We've both been incredibly busy, and I didn't want to add to your worries. However, after receiving the urn with your name, I realized I couldn't delay any longer. I'll report it, I promise."

Moa fiddled with her napkin; her expression unreadable. She opened her mouth as if to speak, but hesitated. Instead, she focused on the fireplace, watching the flames crackle and the occasional sparks pop against the fire guard.

"I'll draft a report," Fredrik said, breaking the silence. "The HR guy seemed experienced, and apparently, I'm not the first person to handle something like this. But still—being accused of rape? That's serious."

Moa's gaze flicked back to him, her eyes filled with concern, but she stayed silent, allowing the weight of the situation to settle between them.

"You're right, unfortunately. As long as the complainant remains anonymous, the best thing to do is to try to stay calm."

Before Fredrik could respond, his phone screen lit up with a new message.

I know where you are.

"Have you ever replied?"

"No, I haven't even thought about it. It seems like a waste of time, doesn't it?"

"Maybe. However, it could be worth trying to see what unfolds."

Fredrik shook his head and turned off his phone, slipping it into his pocket. "I'm not interested in playing cat-and-mouse games."

The door swung open, allowing a rush of chilly air and the hum of the street outside to enter. Jake stepped inside, accompanied by an elegantly dressed woman. Both wore sharp business attire, clearly on their way to or from a meeting.

"He's working late," Moa remarked, nodding toward Jake. "That's one of the city council's lawyers. She's highly competent, well-liked, and even ran for mayor a few years ago."

Jake scanned the room, his gaze landing on Moa and Fredrik. "Have you seen Rune?" he asked. "We were supposed to meet him here but got delayed."

"Unfortunately, no," Moa replied.

Jake and the lawyer settled at the table next to them, pulling out a stack of papers. Despite himself, Fredrik focused on their conversation, noticing that Moa was equally engaged. They discussed the summer plans for the scout club, which included a sailing trip aimed at helping young offenders find a new path.

Fredrik leaned back toward Moa, drawing her attention to their table. "We still need to finalize our travel plans," he said, steering the conversation in a lighter direction.

"And let's focus on the rest of our lives. Time is flying by," Moa replied, her tone tinged with weariness. "Once I sell the house, I might start looking for something more permanent. What do you think? Should I wait and see how the housing market plays out?"

"It's a big decision—and a lot of money—so it's hard to advise you. Plus, you mentioned traveling with Tomas and possibly finding alternative housing for him. It all adds up," Fredrik replied thoughtfully.

Moa grimaced, her frustration bubbling over. "Millions are poured into correctional rehabilitation programs while healthcare services are gutted. And if you want top-notch care when you need it, you must pay out of pocket."

She punctuated her words by dolloping a generous heap of cream onto the last piece of pie, nearly spitting the sentence out.

"Sorry," she muttered, her voice softening. "I'm tired. You know how it is."

Fredrik reached across the table and gave her hand a reassuring squeeze.

The fire in the hearth was dwindling, its warmth dissipating. Nearby, Jake and the lawyer sipped their beers, engrossed in conversation about the upcoming summer season. Fredrik's mind drifted to an image of himself and Moa, consumed by late-night work, skipping workouts, and falling asleep on the couch with the remote in hand—life slowly becoming a grind.

Moa yawned, pulling him back to reality. It was nearly half past ten when Jake and the lawyer had gathered their papers.

"Well, if Rune shows up unexpectedly, let him know we're about to file a missing person report for him," Jake joked, loosening his tie and unbuttoning the top button of his shirt. "I'm heading to check on the warehouse. You never know if these protests will escalate. Who knows—Rune might have fallen asleep at his new office."

Jake chuckled, slipped on his coat, and stepped out into the night.

CHAPTER THIRTY-SEVEN

MOA CURSED HERSELF for not informing Fredrik about Vilda's warning to be careful and about the disturbing incident with the tailgater. Life felt like a chaotic swirl of events, and she struggled to tie up all the loose ends. She even began questioning Vilda's credibility, wondering who she worked for.

Despite the stress and fatigue weighing her down, Moa enjoyed seven hours of sleep—a rare reprieve. She arrived at the hospital parking lot at half past five, allowing herself over an hour of quiet time with her mother before the day's chaos resumed.

The heavy, dry air in the hospital burned her lungs, forcing her to take shallow breaths to avoid the pervasive sense of sickness and death. Even the sterile environment seemed to amplify the distinct body odors of each person she passed, causing her stomach to churn.

Inside Vera's room, the calm rhythm of her mother's breathing filled the air. Her eyes flickered, glossy and distant, and the lines around her mouth had deepened. Moa couldn't help but think back to before the illness when Vera spoke about having fillers and making a fresh start, dreaming of going to the gym and traveling to Greece.

"We'll keep her until tomorrow," a nurse said, his tone indifferent as he avoided eye contact with Vera and Moa.

The scene twisted something within Moa. What her mom had dreaded most had come to pass—she was bedridden, her autonomy stripped away. People spoke about her as if she weren't even there, and her life no longer belonged to her.

The nurse hurried away before Moa could gather her thoughts, leaving her feeling overwhelmed. Vera's weary gaze conveyed everything Moa already understood: What's the point of living when you're dying anyway?

"I..." Vera began, her breath quickening as she attempted to sit up. The movement tugged at the IV connected to her right hand.

Moa's eyes roamed the sterile room, where the only burst of color came from the oxygen valve on the wall—a bright blue, or perhaps sky blue, as a witness might describe it in a statement. Outside, the windows remained dark, the city still shrouded in night. Moa's stomach grumbled, interrupting the silence.

"Moa. You're doing great," Vera murmured, her voice slurred and weak. She sank back into the pillows, her muscles going slack. Moa realized with a jolt that her mother's voice would soon fall silent forever.

Moa squeezed her hand, noticing that her nails were long, uneven, and needed care.

"I brought some new clothes for Tomas," she said, her words flowing as if on autopilot.

Vera closed her eyes, too weak to respond. Moa's mind churned as she desperately searched for something meaningful to say, something that mattered. But her thoughts were tangled in the chaos of recent weeks—death, misery, and endless financial burdens. She had no words left, only the ache of everything unsaid.

A faint smile flickered across Vera's thin face as a phone rang somewhere in the hallway. The scent of coffee drifted into the room, and Moa stood up to pour herself a glass of water, hoping it would stave off her hunger for the time being.

Vera had drifted into sleep, and Moa debated whether to leave. No matter what she did, she felt powerless; there was nothing she could do to ease her mother's suffering. Yet, despite the weight of it all, Moa knew she still needed to manage her own life, starting with the necessity of a proper breakfast to keep herself going.

Instead of leaving immediately, she pulled up a chair, sat down, and took her mother's frail hand. Vera's fingers offered the faintest squeeze, a weak but meaningful connection. The dim lighting in the room deepened Moa's fatigue; she could have fallen asleep right there, whether standing or sitting.

By half-past six, Moa gently tucked Vera's hand under the blanket, kissed her forehead, and decided to bring Tomas on her next visit. She would do whatever was necessary to ensure her mother felt supported. Spending time with someone in need, she believed, was one of the greatest gifts one could give.

Dr. Alicia had reassured Moa that she shouldn't feel guilty if she couldn't visit every day. Vera had been given sedatives and anti-anxiety medication to help keep her calm, and the staff would call if there were any changes. Even so, leaving her mother's side was never easy.

As Moa stepped out of the hospital, she felt a wave of gratitude for the simple relief of leaving—for the chance to walk away, even briefly, into the outside world.

* * *

The staff room at the station was eerily quiet, a rare moment of calm before the inevitable storm. Moa embraced the stillness, savoring the breakfast she had grabbed on her way back from the hospital. Her mind drifted to a different life—one far removed from crime. She imagined herself as a receptionist with steady hours, a chic uniform, and elegant heels. In her daydream, mornings began with checking the news, sipping coffee, and planning the week in a sleek leather-bound planner.

Her thoughts were interrupted by the echoing footsteps in the corridor, the opening and closing of a door, and the crackle of the police radio reporting a traffic accident.

Fredrik's voice filtered in from afar. Moa briefly closed her eyes, holding onto the fleeting tranquility.

"You're early," Fredrik said, jolting her back to reality. "I saw your car. Jake discovered Rune beaten and unconscious in his office at the warehouse, and there has been vandalism."

"At Jake's office?" Moa asked, her brows furrowing.

The police radio buzzed once more, relaying updates: an ambulance was en route to the old port, patrols were requested to secure the area, and bystanders were advised to maintain their distance.

"No, Rune's office is the one that's a mess," Fredrik clarified. "It seems like there's been a break-in. Jake's and Rune's offices have been affected, and the protests last night appear to have escalated. The patrol on the scene is sending Jake here to provide a statement. Also, there's a storm warning accompanying dangerously low temperatures."

Before Moa could reply, Erik walked in briskly. "Good thing you're early, Moa. We're heading out now. I've called for a K-9 unit."

The room's tranquility disappeared, giving way to the urgency of the day's escalating chaos.

CHAPTER THIRTY-EIGHT

JAKE'S SHARP, tailored suit was a striking contrast to the stark environment of the station. For a moment, with the door to the interrogation room ajar, it almost seemed as if Jake himself was in custody. His eyes were bloodshot, but it was impossible to determine whether it was the relentless wind of the Friland Islands or tears—or perhaps both.

"Thanks for coming. I see you have some coffee," Fredrik said, gesturing toward the cup in Jake's hand as he sat down.

Meanwhile, Grim and his team began reviewing surveillance footage from the dock area and the offices of Jake and Rune. Fredrik felt a surge of gratitude for the first patrol on the scene, who acted quickly to maintain the crime scene's integrity and create a clear understanding of the events.

Moa and Erik sent photos of where Rune was found and the graffiti sprayed across the walls of the vandalized offices. The pieces were starting to come together, but questions still loomed.

"When you left The Norse Inn last night, you said you'd be stopping by the office at the dock around half-past ten, right?" Fredrik inquired, leaning forward slightly.

"That's right," Jake replied, his tone steady. "I stopped by to check the doors. Rune rents his new office from me, so we take turns keeping an eye on it, especially since there's been a string of break-ins lately. His car wasn't there, and the door was locked. I knocked a few times, but when no one answered, I went home. He's forgotten about meetings before, it's not unusual. Rune's got too much on his plate these days."

"So, why did you return to the warehouse this morning?"

"The demonstration last night made me uneasy, so I wanted to ensure nothing had been damaged. These situations can spiral out of control, especially when people start drinking. I went down before seven and noticed that my door and Rune's were unlocked. It was clear we had been broken into."

Jake's explanation was clear and concise, and his professional demeanor carried a hint of unease. Lawyers always have a knack for getting to the essentials.

"I checked my office first; it was evident that someone had been there. Then, I went to Rune's office and found him on the floor."

Jake paused, his gaze drifting down the corridor. He took a slow sip of his coffee, blinking back tears. "Will he pull through?"

Fredrik hesitated, recalling the scant information he had from the patrol assisting the ambulance crew. Rune's pulse was weak, and his head injuries were severe.

"It's too early to know for sure," Fredrik said cautiously. "We'll need to wait for updates as the day progresses. Regarding the graffiti saying Preserve Friland, what's your theory?"

Jake straightened, composing himself. "The only thing that comes to mind is that this is a targeted message against business owners. Regardless of our actions, we're seen as the villains. We're blamed for environmental damage. Yet, many people involved in these protests seek an adrenaline rush. Anything they don't immediately grasp turns into a source of anger for them."

His voice was calm, but the frustration behind his words was clear. Fredrik made a mental note to explore the message and the messengers more deeply.

"What's your theory on this?" Fredrik asked, his pen hovering above his notebook.

Jake leaned back in his chair. "I own properties and run several successful businesses, automatically making me a target. We're all lumped together, labeled as capitalists, and blamed for environmental damage. It's frustrating. Take the U.S. for example; three hundred and seventeen tons of tires are discarded yearly. What my company contributes is barely a drop in the ocean, but at least we're trying. I even run a related charity, but it doesn't matter.

People like this rarely look beyond their narrow concerns."

"When did you last see Rune?"

Jake tapped his fingers on the table as he reminisced. "Around eight o'clock last night, he was in his office at the warehouse. I stopped by to pick up a drill I kept there, and reminded him about the meeting later that evening. Nothing seemed unusual. He was his usual self, discussing the storm warning and mentioning that he still needed to check on one of the boats, Aurora. He hadn't managed to get it ashore yet."

Fredrik jotted down the details, mentioning the boat, sparking another thread of questions to follow.

* * *

Fredrik maintained constant communication with Moa and Erik, who had discovered several sets of shoe prints at the warehouse. The tracks seemed amateurish and left carelessly, with no effort to conceal them. Meanwhile, Rune was in a medically induced coma, and his prognosis appeared grim. Forensic pathologist Ida Steen had prepared a preliminary report on his injuries to help Moa and Erik narrow their search.

A patrol officer had briefly interviewed Rune's wife at the hospital. She explained that her husband often worked late, and after taking a sleeping pill, she went to bed, assuming he would return as usual. Panic set in when she woke up and realized he hadn't come home. Despite her shock, she was fully cooperative, and the police were retrieving Rune's call logs and examining his devices.

Fredrik found no prior offenses on Rune's criminal record, so he began piecing together the final hours before the attack. Grim sent an update: the surveillance cameras at Rune's and Jake's offices had been turned off at exactly seven o'clock and remained offline. The system was controlled via an app, raising questions about who had access. According to Moa and Erik, Rune hadn't stored anything of significant value at the premises, which were mainly intended for storage and possibly for upcoming sailing courses with the scouts.

Fredrik broadened his focus, delving deeper into Jake Lund's background. His search uncovered eight companies linked to Jake, from cleaning services to security firms. Jake owned five vehicles, a villa in Toft, two summer houses in Breda, and three racehorses.

"I'm missing something," Fredrik muttered, staring at the screen.

Outside, the wind howled, tugging at a metal sign that creaked as it started to come loose from its mounting.

Fredrik returned to his research, digging deeper into Jake's recycling company. The website emphasized its link to a charitable organization, Tires of Hope, which collected discarded tires from Scandinavia for recycling. The promotional material featured statistics and a photo of the Breda port, where Jake stored several containers to save time when the port in Toft was at capacity.

Digging deeper, Fredrik uncovered further connections. Jake sat on the boards of several housing associations, including Rune's. Additionally, a news blog reported that Breda's municipality was in negotiations to sell the limestone quarry to Jake Lund.

The puzzle became increasingly complex, yet Fredrik was resolute in fitting the pieces together.

CHAPTER THIRTY-NINE

MOA REMOVED HER FACE mask and stretched her legs, wincing at the stiffness from crawling on her knees. She and Erik followed their standard grid pattern, combing the crime scene inch by inch. Despite the heated room, a biting chill seeped under the door, causing her nose to run relentlessly. She felt thirsty, desperate to pee, and even more desperate for the case to make sense.

"Large boots, probably size forty-six." Erik pointed to a footprint. "I don't see any signs of a struggle here. Rune must've been caught off guard. Odd, though, considering how loud that metal door squeaks. Maybe it was someone he knew? Someone he expected to see?"

Moa's eyes scanned the floor. "According to Ida, Rune was struck about thirty times, heavy blows. The scene appears chaotic at first glance, but I suspect it's a setup. Whoever did this intended to mislead us. Consider the scattered pens beneath the desk as an example. They seem to be a calculated distraction. Meanwhile, the rest of the office is oddly tidy. There are no signs of a robbery, and nothing seems to be missing. Just a lot of graffiti on the walls."

Erik squatted by another set of scuff marks. "Whoever overpowered Rune must have been strong. He was a robust guy. Thirty solid blows like that require serious muscle and precision. The first hit must have been decisive; they didn't move far during the attack."

Rune's office appeared stark compared to Jake's. Bare cement walls enclosed a few metal shelves and a small office setup in the corner. Four surveillance cameras were mounted in each corner of the ceiling, capturing every angle. It would have been nearly impossible for anyone to move undetected.

The heavy metal door at the front stood unlocked, and Moa glanced at the smaller wooden door that separated Rune's office from Jake's. The scene felt intentionally constructed, like a puzzle where half the pieces had been swapped.

Moa blew her nose with a crumpled tissue she found in her pocket. They worked quietly, taking turns to photograph and collect evidence. Meanwhile, a patrol team searched Rune's office in Toft, gathering all electronic devices.

Erik's phone rang, shattering the silence. He listened intently, his expression changing from surprise to relief. "They've stopped a stolen Skoda," he said. "A baton was found in the back seat. The driver was an undocumented immigrant, high as a kite, cruising the outskirts of Toft."

"Did they mention the car's color?" Moa asked, her brow furrowing.

"Black."

Her pulse quickened. "That might be the same car that attempted to ram me. I need to report this to Fredrik."

"You should. And if there's anything else you haven't mentioned, now is the time to bring it up."

Moa's phone buzzed. She hoped it was Fredrik with an update from the maritime police, providing her with an easy way to segue into the Skoda lead. But it wasn't Fredrik; it was Dr. Alicia.

Your mother is having severe breathing problems. You should come during the day.

Moa's heart sank. She decided to visit the hospital during her lunch break, aware that they would have to return to the warehouse later in the day. Time was slipping through her fingers.

"We'll take a break soon," she told Erik. "I'll speak to Fredrik once we're back at the station. It's just... a bit overwhelming right now."

Erik agreed, already dialing the electrician from the company that had installed the surveillance cameras. They needed to determine if the system could have been disabled without Rune noticing.

Moa's eyes drifted toward the blood-spattered floor. Crime scene markers stood in stark contrast to the chaos, emphasizing key pieces of evidence. The wall and electrical panel bore smudges of soot, remnants of the crime's aftermath.

She donned a pair of shoe covers and passed gloves to Erik, who was already advancing to the next task. The day was far from over, and the clock continued its relentless march.

"I need to cut the power here for a few minutes, but it seems this unit is on its own circuit," the technician said as she worked. She glanced at Erik and added, "You know this unit shares an app with the one next door, right?"

"Well, now we know," Erik said, sharing a glance with Moa.

The technician moved swiftly, inspecting the unit with practiced efficiency. "Nothing here appears damaged or tampered with," she said, methodically checking the electrical panels and fuse boxes of both offices. Finally, she settled into a corner to review the app's settings on her tablet.

After a few minutes of quick navigation through the app, she announced, "The app is shared between two units. I'll print out the details, including the unit names. The one labeled Rune 1 has never accessed the app, but Jake Office W shows recent activity."

"Could you turn on the cameras now so we can run a test?" Erik suggested.

The wooden door separating the offices groaned as Erik attempted to open it. He stepped to the other side, cracked the door open slightly, and extended his arm toward the nearest camera unit.

"This is the door Jake mentioned he used to check on Rune," Erik said. "The front door hinges were faulty, and with the strong wind, he didn't want to take the chance."

"I see you on two cameras," the technician confirmed. "Now, try the front door."

Erik approached the front door and opened it just enough to reach his arm outside.

"Same result," the technician said, nodding as she clicked her screen. "The cameras are detecting you."

"Excellent," Moa said. "So we can rule out the possibility of someone breaking in to manually disable the cameras. And the power wasn't cut?"

"No, a power cut would have been logged on our end," the technician replied. "The cameras were turned off via the app, and both the user and our system log every instance. It's the user's responsibility to report any issues."

Moa exhaled, a wave of relief washing over her. At last, they were making significant progress.

CHAPTER FORTY

THE MAN IN THE CELL sat huddled, his legs pulled tightly beneath him as he rocked back and forth. His frail body trembled, and his dark eyes darted nervously around the room. The only word he had uttered so far was "Babacar," which he used while pointing to himself. His clothes were grimy, and he carried no identification—neither a driver's license nor an ID card. When presented with a series of flags, he hesitated before pointing to the Senegalese flag.

Fredrik waited nearby for an interpreter.

"We found traces of cocaine in his system, along with alcohol in his blood," said prosecutor Anna, her voice firm as she entered the meeting room with Fredrik. "During the strip search, they found a bag of cannabis on him. What's your take? Do you think this guy could have dumped Benny and his car in the sea, shot Tore, and broken into Rune's office without being seen?"

Fredrik shook his head, his expression resolute. "Not a chance. He can barely stand. My guess? He's a pawn in a larger game."

Anna's lips pressed into a thin line as she considered his words. "Regardless, I'm detaining him for driving under the influence of drugs, suspected vandalism, reckless driving, burglary, and assault. However, I also want him to be checked by a doctor and given food immediately."

Fredrik turned toward the noticeboard. His eyes scanned the expanding collection of notes and photos as he attempted to piece everything together. At the center was a picture of Rune, surrounded by scrawled connections. Next, Fredrik added a summary of Jake's background—details he believed might be vital to the investigation.

The web was becoming more tangled, and the answers seemed out of reach. Yet, Fredrik knew the pieces were beginning to form a picture, and it was just a matter of time.

"What about Jake? Does he have an alibi?" Anna asked, pacing back and forth near the window.

"He's been cooperative and appears genuinely shocked," Fredrik replied. "But whether his reaction is authentic is difficult to determine."

Fredrik rearranged the photos on the board, pausing to update Anna about Jake's late visit to the pub the night before. He scribbled *Babacar?* on a note and pinned it next to Rune's photo. The unanswered questions were piling up, but he resisted the urge to interrupt Grim, who was focused on call lists and messages from Rune's phone. A meeting with Erik and Moa was already scheduled for the afternoon.

Back in his office, Fredrik settled down to draft the report about his stalker for the beige-suited HR manager. However, his thoughts were scattered as he awaited updates from Moa, Erik, and Grim. Meanwhile, a new patrol had begun door-knocking in the port area, questioning neighbors and reviewing surveillance footage from the protest.

Fredrik's attention drifted to the open tabs on his screen—Jake's company and its affiliated charity, Tires of Hope, based in Dakar. On a whim, he typed the charity's address into Google Maps. The street view immersed him in a world of pothole-ridden roads and missing sidewalks. Tin shacks crowded the area, one of which was meant to house the charity's school. When he searched the address listed for their office, he found only an empty crossroads with no buildings in sight.

Feeling a spark of curiosity—and suspicion—Fredrik reached out to the Finnish Mission Society in Senegal. He composed a quick request, asking if anyone could verify the charity's address in Dakar. As he hit send, he couldn't shake the sense that Jake's spotless reputation might have some cracks.

* * *

Fredrik couldn't decide whether investigating Jake's connections to Dakar was worth the time he should have dedicated to finishing his report for the personnel department. Only time would reveal which was more important. He couldn't be in two places at once; there was no way to create a clone of himself.

As usual, Grim was the last to arrive at the meeting room, immediately reaching for a Friland pastry Hanna had brought.

"Are you backtracking on the diet?" Erik teased.

"I skipped lunch," Grim said between bites. "There's too much to do."

Moa jumped in without hesitation. "Someone attempted to run me off the road the other night."

Fredrik's adrenaline surged.

"A black Skoda," Moa continued. "I filed a report right away and submitted the dashcam footage. It was dark, but I'm almost certain the driver was fair-skinned. Before that, I had received a warning from Vilda—you know her, the private investigator. She always advises me to be careful, although she primarily deals with petty crimes, or at least suspicions of them."

"And now?" Erik asked, his tone wary.

Fredrik experienced a pang of unease at the mention of Vilda. Her involvement could complicate matters, particularly if it intersected with their case.

"Jake's wife hired her," Moa explained. "Apparently, Jake's wife suspected he was having an affair. She mentioned that he came home late, smelled of alcohol, and wasn't behaving like himself."

Fredrik stiffened. If Jake became a suspect, Vilda's involvement could complicate Moa's situation.

"The last thing Vilda told me was that she had been threatened and planned to leave for a while. But it's not the first time this has happened. I suggested that she return to the police; things have improved since she left. She would be better protected."

Erik leaned back in his chair, contemplating. "We'll keep your car here, Moa. I'll have someone assess the dent and compare it with the Skoda. For now, you can take a civilian car home tonight. This isn't your fault, and no one could have predicted it. Use the white Toyota—we share it with the digital forensics team."

Moa reached for a pastry. The tension in the room was palpable, yet Erik's calm and steady demeanor helped ease the edge. Grim cleared his throat, brushed the crumbs from his mouth, and began. "Jake's account of repeatedly calling Rune checks out. Rune's phone has the surveillance camera app installed, but he has never used it. It was installed three weeks ago, and the decision to tap his phone has proven effective. Last night at seven, Jake called Rune, asking him to come down to the warehouse before their scheduled meeting with the lawyer, stating he wanted to discuss a few things. At the exact same time, the surveillance cameras in Rune's office were turned off. According to the electrician you brought in, the app had two users: Rune and Jake. And guess who used the app last night at seven? Jake."

The room fell silent, the weight of the revelation pressing down. Fredrik could feel the shift—exhausted faces now infused with renewed energy. The case had taken a sharp, unsettling turn.

"Jake? How could he be so foolish as to make such a mistake?" Anna snapped, her tone icy. "Can we bring him in right away? We need more evidence linking him to the crime, but we can't afford to waste time."

Moa chimed in. "Everything has been sent to the lab, including the baton. We have flagged it as a priority—it's the best we can do for now."

"What about the interpreter?" Erik asked.

"She should arrive this afternoon," Fredrik replied. "In the meantime, Babacar has been sent to the hospital for a check-up—he's completely exhausted."

Fredrik's screen lit up.

"It's the maritime police," he declared, raising a hand to silence the room.

The team froze, with anticipation hanging thick in the air.

"They've discovered what they think is a dumping ground at the coordinates we provided. They're deploying a submersible and working around the clock. We should have answers soon."

The atmosphere in the room shifted once more, now charged with the promise of a breakthrough.

CHAPTER FORTY-ONE

VERA WAS PLACED in a single room in the infection ward—windowless and stark. Dr. Alicia had already briefed Moa over the phone.

"She's sleeping. The night was... fine, I guess," said a young woman at the reception desk, her tone flat and disinterested.

The receptionist was about Moa's age, but her noticeable disinterest in her job was disheartening.

"Your mom had some trouble breathing earlier, but it seems fine now," she added, twirling a pen between her fingers. "I just started my shift, so I don't know much. Someone else should be here soon if you want more details. We have our hands full, so we had to move your mom. It's probably temporary."

"Will someone have time to help her wash later?" Moa asked, although she already knew the answer.

The girl shrugged, her long, false eyelashes fluttering lazily. "Maybe. It depends on the schedule."

Moa felt a familiar wave of anger. Every time, she had to ask, to nag, to ensure her mother received even the most basic care. When they said they had their hands full, it usually meant no space, no time, and no resources. People like the receptionist reminded Moa exactly why she dreaded the thought of her mother being stuck in the system. Budget cuts and apathetic staff forced families to step in and fill the gaps.

She steeled herself, put on a gown, face mask, and gloves, and sanitized her hands.

The stale air hit her immediately, carrying a mix of disinfectants and something heavier. The room resembled a supply closet more than a space intended for a patient. Boxes were stacked haphazardly in one corner, while rolls of paper and white boxes of protective gloves cluttered a stainless-steel bench.

Someone had set up a screen on one side of the bed to shield her from the worst mess. At least Vera wouldn't have to witness the chaos. The walls were freshly painted, and a small night lamp emitted a faint, soothing glow.

Grateful for even the smallest comforts, Moa moved closer to the bed.

"Mom," she whispered softly.

Tears threatened to spill as Moa's throat tightened, leaving her mouth dry as sand. Life wasn't supposed to end like this. Vera's thin eyelids fluttered, her once-pristine lashes now bare, lacking the Dior mascara she had applied every morning without fail. Vera had never gone a day without showering.

When Moa and Tomas begged for camping trips and tent-sleeping, Vera firmly refused. She preferred a proper hotel, a large bathroom, and comfort. Over time, Moa stopped arguing and eventually learned to appreciate the same comforts her mother cherished.

Gently, she stroked Vera's cheek, now hollow and fragile. Her mother's face had grown sharper, her nose taking on that pointed look Moa knew all too well; it was the undeniable sign of time running out. She prayed Vera wouldn't have to die in this makeshift storage room. Her hand hovered over her phone, tempted to call Dr. Alicia, but she stopped herself. Alicia had already finished her shift, and room assignments weren't her responsibility anyway.

Despite the grim situation, the only glimmer of hope was that someone else might pass away, freeing up a better room, preferably one with a view. It was a harsh thought, but Vera deserved dignity. So much remained undone—trips, plans, dreams postponed with excuses, Moa recognized too well. Time is always too short, and there is too much to do. Moa could see herself walking the same path, chasing time, burning herself out, and one day ending her life in a room like this.

"If you want more information," the girl at reception had said earlier. About what? About what it's like to die in a glorified closet?

At least Kajsa was on her way and planned to stay until the evening. The thought brought Moa a flicker of relief, easing her spiraling anxiety.

The door creaked open as a nurse pushed in a medicine cart. He greeted her with a quiet, "Good morning." His voice was mechanical, and his movements were efficient. Without saying a word, he checked off a list, adjusted the IV, and administered an injection through the catheter in Vera's hand.

He offered Moa a smile, but she could see the apology reflected in his weary eyes. 'I only work here; it's not my fault that your mom is dying in this room.'

And yet, whether it was a fault or not, the weight of the indignity settled heavily in Moa's chest.

As he left, the nurse accidentally bumped the cart into a stack of boxes, causing them to wobble precariously. The door closed, sealing the stale air once again.

Outside, the sun shone brightly, life went on, and Moa recognized she was one of the fortunate ones who could leave. Vera, however, was among the unfortunate—she would never again experience the warmth of a beautiful day or the promise of a fresh start.

A fresh wave of anxiety swept over Moa. She had been too hard on herself lately. There was still a chance, however slim, that she wouldn't develop ALS. Maybe she could still live a comfortable life, traveling regularly with Tomas as planned.

Kajsa interrupted her spiraling thoughts as she entered the room, wearing a face mask. Her dark eyes smiled warmly, offering a sense of comfort that Moa already knew she would miss when Vera was gone. Though their relationship had evolved into a friendship, Kajsa had a new job that would soon occupy most of her time.

Moa had considered hiring Kajsa part-time as an assistant for Tomas. When the time came for their first trip, Tomas would require professional help and someone to plan suitable activities for him. Although the staff at the rehabilitation facility were kind and competent, Tomas needed a connection to the outside world, someone who didn't spend their days walking those same corridors. Kajsa's services would come at a cost, but Moa was confident she could manage it.

"I'll take it from here," Kajsa said, slipping off her coat. "I brought some food. I see they've booked her into the suite."

"I heard it's just temporary," Moa replied.

"I'll keep you updated. It should be quieter now. Alicia mentioned that the antibiotics are starting to work. Maybe this room isn't such a bad idea—it's peaceful, at least."

Moa approached her mother's bedside, took her hand, and squeezed it gently, hoping for a response. However, her mother's hand remained cold and limp. Moa carefully tucked it under the blanket.

She felt torn; part of her wanted to stay, while another part longed to leave. Her conscience urged her to stay, help wash her mother, endure hours in the unforgiving chair by the bed, and make do with a packed lunch from a plastic container. But logic reminded her that there was nothing more she could do. Vera would likely sleep through the night.

"Mom, I'll be back," she whispered. "Kajsa is here with you."

Moa needed fresh air and a bottle of water. She hugged Kajsa, who placed a reassuring hand on her arm and said, "Call me if you need anything."

As Moa stepped out of the room, she felt relief in leaving the suffocating confines of what felt like a morgue.

CHAPTER FORTY-TWO

THE FLOW OF INFORMATION surged throughout the day, keeping Fredrik on his toes as he moved between the meeting room and his office. The information on the noticeboard shifted constantly, as if rearranging itself to reveal the larger picture. With an afternoon meeting on the horizon, Fredrik felt a growing sense of confidence—they were close to solving the case. The final pieces of the puzzle were nearly within reach.

The first report from the maritime police was both shocking and ominous. It detailed an unsettling discovery of dumped tires and containers at the site. Even more chilling were indications of human remains among the debris. The contents of the containers remained a mystery, but early suspicions pointed to environmental toxins. Additional personnel were urgently needed, prompting the deployment of boats and specialized equipment from Norway. Before retrieval efforts could commence, the team needed to ensure there were no immediate leaks and devise a safe recovery plan. The entire operation would incur a staggering cost.

Meanwhile, Jake's phone stayed silent, and an arrest warrant was issued in absentia. His wife, during interrogation, vehemently denied any involvement or knowledge of what she referred to as his "double life." She asserted that she had never set foot in Dakar, claiming to manage the charity's administration entirely from home.

The meeting room buzzed with quiet energy as Fredrik's colleagues gathered, coffee cups in hand. The air was thick with expectation, every glance and whispered conversation charged with anticipation of a breakthrough in the case.

As usual, Grim was the last to arrive, slightly out of breath.

"I've reviewed this sequence from the maritime police with Grim several times," Fredrik began, pulling up a radar video on the giant screen displaying the marine traffic. Rune's yacht appeared as a purple triangle, departing the port in Toft nearly at the same time as one of Jake's cargo ships, marked in green. The cargo ship veered sharply off course as both vessels neared the suspected dumping site. Rune's yacht paused briefly in the area before continuing its journey.

"I can't make sense of this," Fredrik admitted, scratching his head. "While working with the maritime police, we mapped the routes based on the dates in Tore's logbook—dates that indicate he was working. We suspect the 'S' in his entries stands for Senegal. But here's the thing: a yacht can't dump large quantities of tires or containers. Maybe Tore was being used as a pilot or somehow overseeing the dumping. He hasn't been away for extended periods lately."

"And Benny—what's his connection to all this? Did he stumble onto something? People talk, rumors spread, and someone always sees more than they're supposed to. Benny's so-called 'warehouse art' wasn't just photography; he spent a lot of time around the port."

Fredrik quickly took a sip of coffee, spilling it on his shirt. Anna silently handed him a napkin.

"Let's move on," he said, clearing his throat. "I've received photos of Jake's supposed office in Dakar. His charity, Tires of Hope, claims to operate from here."

Fredrik clicked to display an image of an empty intersection. "This is the address. The nearest building is half a kilometer away, and there isn't a school. It's all a façade. His wife claims to know nothing, but Grim will update us on her interrogation shortly."

"What we know is that Jake was well compensated to manage the tires responsibly. Rather than recycling them, he disposed of most in the ocean. Evidence indicates the presence of human remains at the site, along with the environmental damage."

The room fell silent as Fredrik's words lingered in the air, the weight of the discoveries bearing down on everyone.

"This might just be the tip of the iceberg," Grim began. "Jake's wife wasn't managing emails personally—she was using a bot to respond. The charity funds? They were channeled through a middleman who later invested in one of Jake's companies, boosting the stock value. You've likely heard of Nordic Wave, the company that's been skyrocketing on the stock market. Well, it's linked to Jake."

A ripple of murmurs spread through the room, punctuated by the scrape of a chair. Anna jotted down notes and interjected, "We have a brief statement from Babacar. He was terrified, high, and disoriented—but there was a hint of relief in him. Furthermore, his testimony is unraveling a larger web of human trafficking."

She turned to Fredrik, who continued.

"Babacar was one of many who paid an exorbitant price to reach Europe. He had heard stories of others who made the journey and secured better lives, so his family took out a loan to send him. However, when he realized they were crammed into a shipping container on one of Jake's vessels, he panicked and found a way to hide onboard.

"Babacar has identified both Rune and Tore. He claims that Rune found him hiding and permitted him to stay on one of the boats—until Jake became aware of it. That's when things escalated. Babacar overheard their shouting. Jake promised him money but also made chilling threats, stating he'd kill Babacar's family if he didn't comply with orders."

Fredrik paused, his expression tense. He reached for a glass of water, took a slow sip, and stood to gather his thoughts—the weight of their discoveries hung heavily in the room.

"Rune also rendezvoused with the cargo ship at its designated spot after returning from Senegal," Fredrik began, his voice heavy. "On the journey there, they carried legitimate cargo, but on the return trip, they dumped refugees at various locations. Babacar revealed that he was present on one of those occasions, working to pay off his mounting heroin debt. The debt kept spiraling, increasing every single day.

"They coerced some refugees into working as seamen during the voyage. Tore supervised the disposal. After seizing their phones, they cast the refugees overboard. Babacar's responsibility was to update the statuses on the victims' phones to create the illusion that they were thriving in Europe."

"They screamed," Moa interjected, her voice breaking slightly. "Just as Tore wrote in his logbook. And then Babacar updated their phones?"

"For God's sake!" Erik shouted, rising abruptly and slamming his hand on the table. "Excuse me."

He left the room without looking back. Fredrik caught a glimpse of tears in Erik's eyes. Turning to the team, he said, "I feel the same way. Honestly, I haven't processed everything yet. I'll definitely need a few therapy sessions when this case is finally closed."

"Handshake," Moa said suddenly, gesturing toward the radar image on the screen. "Could the boats be swapping their AIS signals?"

Grim stood up, narrowing his eyes as he examined the screen. "You're right," he said.

"I'll check on Erik," Anna said as she left the room.

Fredrik glanced at Moa, approval evident in his expression. "Let's wait for Erik to return before we continue. I'll get some coffee. Take a few minutes to regroup."

A handwritten note featuring Jake's name now sat prominently at the top of the noticeboard.

Grim pointed to the radar sequence as he explained Moa's theory. "The ships approach one another, exchanging AIS transponder codes or manually altering the AIS data. After completing their task, they revert to their original signals. It's a clever method to evade detection."

"Babacar has been ruled out as the driver of the Skoda," Fredrik said. "In his condition, he couldn't have managed the high speeds needed to run someone off the road. Ida sent an update: he's being admitted for detox. He's experiencing seizures and is severely dehydrated, and they've discovered atrial fibrillation. He probably used the last of his strength to share his version of events. I suspect he still has more to tell us."

"Are you suggesting that Jake attempted to run me off the road?" Moa asked.

"Most likely," Fredrik replied, pacing around the table.

"We have a lot to untangle," he added. "Finding Jake is crucial. I assume he's still carrying the weapon he used on Tore."

"Tore might have started leaking small details to Benny," Moa speculated. "Maybe he tried to reach out to Rune, hoping to gather more information. Jake probably found out and silenced everyone. Tore must have felt terrible about everything; hence the graffiti. It's as if he wanted to tell the world. But who would believe him? An alcoholic sailor or a slick, high-profile lawyer?"

Fredrik paused, then sat down, leaning forward. "As time goes by, Jake digs himself deeper into this mess. I doubt Rune was entirely in agreement with what was happening. Taking in Babacar doesn't scream 'ruthless.' And let's not forget, we were sitting across from Jake at The Norse Inn last night. Dressed in a suit, polished and put-together—it's hard to reconcile that image with what we know now."

He shifted gears. "Rune's boat, Aurora, is still in the port, cordoned off with a patrol standing guard. Can you, Erik, and Moa search it tomorrow?"

Before Moa could respond, her screen lit up with a notification.

"It's the lab," she said. "We have a match on the tire tracks from the cliff. They correspond to the Skoda."

"Good. Let's hope they find Jake quickly. He likely realizes his time is running out."

CHAPTER FORTY-THREE

MOA HELD OUT HER phone to show Tomas a picture of Fredrik. His face brightened with a smile as he reached for it.

"His name is Fredrik," she signed, her movements slow and deliberate. "You, me, and Fredrik—we will find a house together."

Tears pricked Moa's eyes, and she hesitated, overwhelmed by the emotions swirling within her. Exhaustion clung to her, seeping into a part of her soul that no amount of rest could touch. She wanted to be everything Tomas needed while still forging her own path. The investigation had taken a shocking turn, and the thought of the media frenzy when the truth about the island's most prominent lawyer came to light weighed heavily on her. One day, she would share everything with Tomas—her role in unraveling it all. He had always told her how proud he was of her, and those words often fueled her determination to get through her grueling shifts. They reminded her that she was making a difference.

Tomas softly took a napkin from the table and wiped her tears away.

"Together," he said slowly, his voice strained yet filled with intent.

"Yes," Moa replied, her voice shaking. "We'll be strong together. It's just… Everything has been overwhelming lately, with work and Mom. I promise to take care of you."

They clasped hands, her gaze drifting to the scars on his—each one a testament to his strength. She would move mountains for him; she knew that with absolute certainty. Goodness had to prevail; it always did in fairy tales.

"I have to go in a minute," she continued. "Fredrik and I are going out for dinner. We've started talking about the future—after everything with Mom. He really wants to meet you. I think you'd have a lot in common."

Tomas smiled softly, his eyes fluttering shut as he gave her hand another gentle squeeze.

"Together," he whispered.

* * *

Moa brushed her wig, her fingers grazing the tiny hairs sprouting at the edges of her scalp. Despite everything, there was justice in the world, however small.

She had slipped into a clean pair of jeans when a message from Dr. Alicia lit up her phone. Vera was deteriorating, and it was time to come to the hospital for the last time.

Without hesitation, Moa called Fredrik. He listened quietly, asked if she wanted company, offered his support, and reassured her that there would be plenty of opportunities for a night out. Before she could respond, the line went dead.

Moa stared at her phone, her chest tightening with words she wasn't ready to say. She had been moments away from telling him that she loved him.

CHAPTER FORTY-FOUR

THE CANCELED DINNER provided Fredrik the perfect opportunity to investigate the pizza restaurant from which his stalker's orders originated. Despite the biting cold, the door to Nordic Crust Pizza stood ajar. Inside, the sweet aroma of freshly baked pizza mingled with the sharp scent of basil, wafting through the small space with its three humble tables designed for takeout customers.

A young man in a yellow reflective vest stood smoking by the kitchen entrance, casually exhaling into the frosty air. Shouts and laughter echoed from the kitchen, creating a chaotic soundtrack.

Fredrik hesitated, debating whether to show his badge or maintain a casual demeanor. Before he could decide, a familiar voice cut through the noise.

"Fredrik? So you're the pizza king of Toft, hosting pizza parties now?"

Fredrik turned sharply, coming face-to-face with Lars Gaard—Friland's notorious TV chef, known for his fiery outbursts and questionable acquaintances. Their paths had crossed the previous year at a hotel in Nordby.

"Do you work here?" Fredrik asked, quickly realizing how absurd it sounded.

His stained chef's uniform and the white powder dusting his nose and cheeks, which Fredrik assumed was flour this time, answered the question.

"Sure do. Welcome to the Nordic Crust Pizza. The usual?" Lars replied with a smirk.

Fredrik hesitated, gathering his thoughts as the man in the yellow vest extinguished his cigarette on the floor, picked up an order, and whistled as he departed.

"There's been a mix-up," Fredrik said cautiously. "A misunderstanding. Could you provide the number of the person ordering pizzas under my name?"

Lars planted his feet wide and crossed his arms, radiating defiance. Angry voices and the clanging of pots erupted from the kitchen, and moments later, a short man with a shiny bald head burst into the room, wielding a broom. Fredrik caught sight of a brown rat darting under the counter.

"Are you here as a cop or a private citizen?" Lars asked, his tone sharp.

"Private citizen," Fredrik responded, maintaining a neutral expression.

For now.

Lars shrugged and gestured for Fredrik to follow him into a cramped office filled with clutter—a broken chair, a desk overflowing with receipts, and boxes stacked precariously.

"I record all calls for security reasons," Lars said flatly. "You can listen, but don't ask stupid questions. You owe me. Got it?"

He opened a beer and offered one to Fredrik, who politely declined with a shake of his head.

"I get it. Let's start with the most recent call—yesterday," Fredrik said.

Lars retrieved a phone from his pocket, quickly navigated to an audio file, and saved it before forwarding it to Fredrik.

"It's always from an unknown number," Lars muttered. "The voice is odd, as if they're trying to disguise it. People can be strange."

"Did my orders come through via calls?" Fredrik asked.

Lars took a swig of his beer and said, "Yep. We don't do apps. This place is like a factory, a gold mine. I'm flipping pizzas while taking calls."

Fredrik's eyes darted to the open cash box on the desk, where bundles of cash sat loosely stacked. He also observed four surveillance cameras in the corners of the room, their lenses glinting.

"And the payment?" Fredrik asked.

"We have a system for regulars who don't ask too many questions," Lars replied, his tone sly. "It's all managed online through a third party."

Black money. Lots of it.

"Thanks," Fredrik said, maintaining a neutral tone.

"I thought the name sounded familiar, but didn't make the connection," Lars said with a smirk. "Stop by sometime—I'll treat you to pizza or a beer. Remember who your friends are and don't ask too many questions."

As Fredrik left the office, the sweet aroma of pizza soured in his mind. Any appetite he had vanished. On his way out, he resolved to seriously pursue finding an apartment, cooking meals, and adopting a healthier lifestyle.

Fredrik couldn't shake the unsettling feeling that clung to him like a second skin. Lars Gaard might have been illegally recording calls, falsifying records, and barely adhering to health regulations, judging by the state of Nordic Crust. If the authorities caught wind of it, they'd shut the place down instantly. Unsure how to proceed, Fredrik decided to stay put and dig deeper. One thing was clear: he distinctly heard a foghorn and a barking dog in the background during the mysterious call. On Friland, with 288 islands, only six inhabited, and countless ports, foghorns weren't exactly a rare sound.

A cold wind tossed the dry autumn leaves like restless spirits as he rounded the corner onto the cobblestone street leading to The Norse Inn. The pub was dark, the light at the back entrance was out, and the corridor bulb, broken for what felt like ages, remained unfixed despite Fredrik reminding Hanna twice. He considered changing it himself. Wasn't there time for anything anymore? Life seemed to be an endless chase: for tomorrow, for success, for better ratings, for more of everything.

He took the final step into the dim corridor, catching the faint trace of Ingrid's perfume lingering in the air. Perhaps she had returned. She hadn't been herself since the stalking incident, and he made a mental note to check in on her the following day.

Then he heard a faint disruption in the silence. A motion in the darkness.

Fredrik's instincts kicked in as a metallic flash caught his eye. His stomach clenched, and the air was filled with the acrid tang of fear, a potent mix of adrenaline and sweat. It was a scent he recognized well from interrogation rooms when suspects broke under pressure.

Pain flared in his right shoulder as something sharp grazed him. He lunged forward, spun, and raised his arms defensively. In the dim light, he caught sight of the glint of a knife aimed at him. Acting on pure reflex, he struck upward, sidestepping as the blade missed its mark. His left arm hit the wall hard, but his momentum carried him through. With a sharp kick, he sent the metal object flying across the floor.

A thud followed by a scream. *Ingrid!*

Fredrik registered the searing pain in his shoulder but allowed the adrenaline coursing through him to push past it, giving him a surge of strength. Ingrid lay sprawled in front of him, blocking the stairs. Slowly, she rose, unsteady, and directed her phone's flashlight right into his face. The blinding beam left him temporarily disoriented, and his inner voice roared into the void of his confusion.

Lash out, hit her, don't think. Defend yourself, for God's sake.

Her voice sliced through the haze, venomous and brimming with rage.

"You damn cop, you killed my husband."

A mocking laughter followed, sharp and chilling. Instinct kicked in, overtaking Fredrik. For the first time in his life, he lashed out at a woman, kicking hard. His foot connected with her stomach, and Ingrid screamed as the knife clattered to the floor while she stumbled back against the wall. The sound of her retching and gasping for air echoed through the corridor.

Fredrik wasted no time. Tearing off his scarf, he wrapped it around the blade to pick it up, his hands trembling. A warm, sticky sensation spread beneath his jacket, seeping down his back. He pushed through the dizziness, concentrating on each step as he walked toward the street.

His mouth was dry, and his words were thick and sluggish as he dialed 112. He repeated the address twice in an effort to be clear. Behind him, Ingrid's cries morphed into pitiful whimpers, echoing through the dark corridor.

Fredrik crawled onto the street, his body growing weaker with each movement. The cold night air stung his face, creating a harsh contrast to the heat radiating from the spreading blood that soaked his clothes. Blue lights began to flash between the rows of silent houses. He collapsed beneath a streetlamp, clutching the knife tightly wrapped in his scarf. The blue light from the patrol cars mingled with the red glow of the ambulance, painting the world in flashes of urgency. Everything else was still as Fredrik closed his eyes, his final sight, the reflection of spinning lights on the wet asphalt.

CHAPTER FORTY-FIVE

THE COMFORTING AROMA of freshly brewed coffee lingered in the hospital corridor like a soothing veil, a faint attempt to soften the harshness of grief. The receptionist with fake eyelashes had been replaced by a thin, pale young man in a uniform two sizes too large.

Inside Vera's room, a candle flickered softly on the side table. The boxes that once cluttered the floor were neatly covered with a sheet, and someone had even cleared the bench where they had been stacked. It was a small yet thoughtful gesture.

Kajsa placed a comforting hand on Moa's back.

"I'm sorry. She passed away a little while ago," Kajsa said, her voice trembling.

Tears rolled silently down Moa's cheeks as Kajsa gently dabbed at her own with a tissue.

Vera lay peacefully, free of tubes and monitors, dressed in clean pajamas. Once marred by time and pain, her skin now appeared smooth and serene. Her mother's hands were still and cool under Moa's touch, resting gently atop the blanket. She sat on the edge of the bed, stroking them, her mind a whirlwind. She had seen countless lifeless bodies in her line of work, yet now, her mother had joined their ranks.

Sounds of clattering and raised voices filtered in from the corridor—a woman's shrill demands to see a doctor shattering the fragile quiet. The candle by the bedside flickered in its glass holder, its glow trembling like Moa's thoughts. She needed to leave. She needed the sanctuary of her home, the solace of her own space to grieve properly. But the demands of life intruded, her phone buzzing insistently with calls from people unaware that this was the worst possible time.

Kajsa, standing nearby, fumbled through her bag, her hands trembling.

"There were two letters," she said softly, her voice trembling.

She held out two envelopes: one bore the names Moa and Tomas; the other was addressed to Kajsa. The weight of what they might contain settled heavily in the room.

"Your mom gave me these a while ago. I've been carrying them with me ever since," Kajsa said.

Her hand shook as she passed Moa the envelope. Words swirled in her mind; there was so much she wanted to say. Her throat tightened, and she blinked away the sting of tears before leaning down to kiss her mother's cool cheek. Amid the sterile smell of the hospital and the lingering scent of illness, her mother's familiar fragrance broke through the sorrow.

Kajsa's quiet sobs evolved into loud, uncontrollable cries. Moa instinctively wrapped her arms around her, offering solace despite her heartbreak.

The rest blurred into a routine. Moa moved through the final steps with the staff, signing papers and answering a few last questions. They handed her a small bag containing her mother's belongings, its weight feeling heavier than it should. She left the ward and her mother behind.

* * *

At ten o'clock, Moa sank into the couch, exhaustion draping over her like a heavy blanket. She had everything under control. Tomas was informed, and she had managed to eat a quick, ready-made meal.

The envelope remained unopened on the table, a quiet reminder of her mother's final thoughts. The image of her mother recognizing her fading strength brought fresh tears to Moa's eyes. She let the tears fall freely, wiped her nose, and adjusted the pillow behind her neck, trying to steady herself.

Her body felt heavy yet oddly calm, her limbs responding despite the weight of the day's emotions. Slowly, she reached for the envelope, her fingers trembling as she unfolded the letter. Her mother's last words awaited, poised to bridge the silence.

My dear Moa and Tomas,

The end is merely the beginning of something new. Take care of one another. Remember to pause and breathe from time to time. Talk to each other, resolve misunderstandings. Moa, I was never as brave as you. That courage came from your father. I couldn't tell you this before, but my mother and the rest of the family turned their backs on me when I was expecting you. Your father was an exhilarating adventure, full of promises he couldn't keep. One day, he simply vanished. I was alone until Patrik entered my life. He believed you were his, and I also allowed myself to believe it.

Sometimes in life, we must make choices that feel wrong in the moment but are right in the long run. Dear Moa, I ask for your forgiveness. Your biological father's name is Ole Klint. We met one warm summer in Amsterdam. He was Norwegian—a kind man with good intentions and blue eyes. We were young, had no money, and lacked a clear plan for the future. He dreamed of becoming a pilot—perhaps he achieved that dream.

Take care of Tomas, just as you did when he was a newborn, watching over him with such devotion. Never let any man dictate your life choices, Moa. Sell the house, as we discussed. Save some money and travel. Create memories and explore the world together. And don't forget to accept help when it's offered—my beloved children, it's okay to lean on others.

I will miss you deeply, but now I'll be in heaven, watching over you from time to time. I love you both so much. Mom

It was past midnight when Moa locked the front door, and the silence wrapped around her like a heavy blanket. She missed Fredrik's voice—they always talked in the evenings, but not even a message had come through. A wave of loneliness washed over her, making her feel like the loneliest person in the world.

Unable to hold back, she typed him a message.

I love you. Take care of yourself, and sleep well.

Switching off her phone, she curled up on the couch, still dressed, and drifted into a restless sleep.

CHAPTER FORTY-SIX

INGRID JERKED VIOLENTLY in a sudden, desperate attempt to break free. Fredrik caught glimpses of worried expressions on the rescue personnel's faces and Ingrid's pale, contorted visage. Moments ago, she had seemed like a fragile, helpless figure, almost doll-like, but now she appeared to have aged a decade in mere minutes.

She resisted fiercely, shouting as the patrol struggled to guide her into the waiting car. The handcuffs gleamed under the flashing blue lights, while her voice rang out in fury, accusing everyone of deserving to die and labeling the cops as murderers for what happened to her husband.

"Can you hear me?" asked a calm, steady voice. "Stay with us. Don't fall asleep. What's your name?"

Fredrik had been in similar situations countless times, coaching injured people to stay conscious with words of hope and reassurance. But now, it was his turn to be on the receiving end.

He fought to stay awake, muttering his name repeatedly. He listed his blood type, badge number, address, phone number, shoe size, and even his favorite color in an effort to keep talking. His colleagues chuckled softly, their laughter a small attempt to ease the tension.

"You're going to be okay," another voice said reassuringly. "You've been stabbed in the shoulder. You've lost some blood, but we're taking you straight to the ER. We're giving you something for the pain now. Just hang on."

As they lifted him onto the stretcher, Fredrik's thoughts blurred, caught somewhere between the sting of pain and the strange comfort of their words.

A fentanyl patch adhered to his skin, and gradually, the panic, fear, and pain began to fade. Somewhere beyond the fog of his thoughts, Fredrik heard Hanna's distressed voice, echoing faintly before the ambulance doors shut with a firm finality.

* * *

When he opened his eyes, the hospital room was dim, and Hanna slumped in a chair beside his bed, fast asleep. Fredrik moved cautiously, wiggling his toes to test for sensation and motor control. He methodically worked his way through each part of his body, pressing his fingertips together to confirm feeling and scanning for anything amiss.

He took a deep, deliberate breath. No sharp pangs, no tightness—his ribs were mercifully intact. The sterile scent of antiseptics lingered in the air, familiar yet not alarming. Glancing to his side, he noted the steady drip from three IV bottles, likely a cocktail of painkillers and antibiotics. His right shoulder felt uncomfortably taut, encased in a thick bandage. His mind came to the realization.

The right shoulder.

Damn.

Fredrik's mind immediately shifted into analysis mode. He couldn't allow himself to spiral into guilt; there was no way he could have foreseen what Ingrid was capable of. Perhaps not even she had fully grasped her capacity for violence. And Hanna? This night would likely linger in her conscience, a weight she'd bear even though it wasn't her fault. She'd blame herself, but she shouldn't.

Then it hit him.

The foghorn. The dog.

Ingrid had orchestrated everything. She ordered the pizzas, positioning herself as both victim and manipulator, playing her role to perfection. She had deceived everyone, including him. Their connection felt genuine, but it was simply part of her plan.

It wasn't your fault.

A cheerful nurse with freckles peeked into the room, her presence a sharp contrast to the heaviness of his thoughts. She checked his IV line with practiced ease.

"The doctor will be in tomorrow morning to discuss everything," she whispered. "The surgery lasted four hours, but it seems successful. You're breathing well, your vitals are stable, and you're tough. I'll stop by a few more times before my shift ends."

"Thank you," Fredrik replied, glancing at Hanna, who was still asleep in the chair beside him. "Could you put a blanket over her?"

"Of course. The poor thing has been here all night. We gave her a mild sedative—she was so upset but wouldn't leave your side."

The nurse gently draped a thick blue blanket over Hanna and then set a pitcher of water and a couple of glasses on the bedside table. Fredrik was advised not to drink anything for a few hours. After surviving both a gunshot wound and a knife attack, he wasn't about to risk choking on water and turning it into the irony of the century.

His thoughts drifted to Moa. She was likely safe in her bed, blissfully unaware of the chaos that had unfolded just a block from the station. Perhaps she was dreaming of sunny Greek islands, far removed from the storm he had just weathered. Fredrik imagined the future—meeting Tomas, traveling with Moa, building a life together on Friland, and creating memories that would last a lifetime.

He felt a profound sense of calm, safety, and belonging for the first time in years. He was grateful for his colleagues' composure and professionalism in the face of a crisis. As a cop, one learns to control emotions, focus on the facts, and move forward.

Fredrik was determined to see Benny and Tore's cases through to the end. He had risked his life twice for justice, and he wouldn't stop until it was served.

CHAPTER FORTY-SEVEN

ERIK HAD CALLED MOA as soon as she woke, filling her in on the shocking events of the night. Moa wasn't surprised; she had never trusted Ingrid. Later, she spoke with Fredrik, who was exhausted but comforted by the sound of her voice. He mentioned that Hanna had stayed with him through the night. The Norse Inn was now cordoned off, with restricted access until further notice. Moa felt powerless—there was nothing she could do for Fredrik, nor could she alleviate her grief over her mother's passing or the chaos surrounding them.

Erik waited in the car downstairs as Moa prepared for another long day, the last before her three-day break. As always, she buried her struggles beneath the demands of her job, and it worked for her.

"How's Fredrik? Everyone at the station is talking about what happened. Ingrid—she's the last person anyone would suspect," Erik said as she slid into the passenger seat.

"He's exhausted but thankful it wasn't worse. We'll see what the doctor says, but I can't picture how he'll manage another round of sick leave. They'll likely find him some easy desk work at the station so he doesn't feel entirely useless."

"Yeah, no one enjoys sitting at home staring at the walls. Anyway, there's Rune's boat—nice name, Aurora."

A patrol was stamping their feet against the cold at the dock as a sharp wind tugged at the barrier tape.

"Finally, we're freezing out here. Remove the tape when you're ready," one of the officers said before the two-man patrol headed off.

Dark clouds loomed on the horizon as Moa squinted at the dock, which felt lifeless in the cold.

"There are still many private boats here," she noted. "They'd better hurry up and haul them out before winter sets in."

She counted seven boats, three of which were luxury vessels worth a fortune. The deserted area was a far cry from the vibrant summers it once knew. Now, only the whisper of the wind remained, and it was difficult to imagine warm days spent on the sun-drenched wooden deck of the pier.

They boarded at the stern, with Erik hefting the technician's bag into the cabin. As Moa was about to descend, she heard Erik taking a call. The sound of hurried footsteps caught her attention. A man sprinted along the pier, his coat flapping wildly in the wind. She froze, immediately recognizing him. Instinctively, she crouched low, her fingers finding the grip of her weapon as she held her breath, waiting for him to pass.

"Erik!" she hissed, striving to keep her voice both urgent and quiet. "Erik!"

She gestured for him to hurry, then leaped onto the dock. Her foot slipped, causing her to stumble to her knees, pain radiating through her leg as it hit the hard surface. Undeterred, she scrambled to her feet, weapon drawn, and shouted:

"Police! Stop!"

Jake didn't slow down. Instead, he veered toward a nearby boat and leaped aboard.

"Police! Stop, or I'll shoot!" Moa yelled again, her voice slicing through the cold, desolate air.

She advanced cautiously, her weapon trained on him, every nerve in her body coiled. "Cover me, Erik!" she shouted, her voice taut with urgency.

Jake turned abruptly, a weapon now in his hand. Moa reacted instinctively, diving to the side.

A shot cracked through the air, reverberating off the silent, abandoned buildings. The sound sent a flock of seagulls soaring skyward, their wings slicing through the stillness as chaos unfolded below.

Moa rolled onto the pier and jumped into a boat. She felt the warm trickle of blood running down her leg but forced herself to block out the pain, shutting down all emotion. Crouching, she moved forward along the side of the boat, gaining a clear view of Jake, who was about to unlock the cabin. Taking a deep breath, she steadied her aim while supporting the other. The shot rang out, splintering the wood inches from Jake. He screamed, startled, and fired wildly in her direction. Moa didn't flinch. She fired again, her bullet striking his leg. Jake crumpled to the deck with a cry of pain, the weapon slipping from his grasp and disappearing into the water with a splash.

The sirens' wail broke through the tense silence, and moments later, the dock was awash with flashing blue lights. Moa turned, her eyes locking with Erik's steady gaze. He was crouched behind a trash can, his face calm but alert. He raised a thumb in quiet acknowledgment.

Moa noticed the growing pool of blood at her feet and the sharp ache in her knee. Despite the pain, she managed a small, triumphant smile and returned Erik's thumbs-up. The chaos was subsiding. They had Jake, and the situation was under control.

EPILOGUE

THE OPEN FIREPLACE at The Norse Inn crackled softly, filling the room with a comforting warmth that enveloped Fredrik and Moa. They sat together in peaceful silence, absorbing the stillness. Their wounds—both physical and emotional—would heal with time. Justice had been served, but not without a heavy cost.

The pub took on new life, attracting tourists intrigued by the recent events. Hanna had hired extra staff to manage the influx. From Norway, Vilda had reached out, offering crucial information that helped the police untangle the threads of Jake's operation. Under police protection for the foreseeable future, she even promised to find, as Moa put it, a "real job" and would consider returning as a detective inspector.

"These little moments," Moa said, breaking the silence, "are what really matter."

"They're the glue of life," Fredrik agreed, gently squeezing her hand. "They're what holds us together, keeping us sane."

A forgotten game with a die lay on the table between them. Fredrik picked it up, rolling it absently across the wood.

"Sometimes you win, sometimes you lose," he said with a faint smile.

"That's true," Moa replied, her eyes meeting his. "But you can always keep the die in your pocket and take another chance anytime."

THE CLOVER

Book 3 in the Friland Murders series

THE NIGHT SKY blazes with fire. On the beach, cameras zoom in on the burning effigy atop the raft. The opening of the summer festival on the Friland Islands is about to be etched into memory—not with joy, but horror. The event is being livestreamed as the fire warden signals the start of the fireworks.

A scream cuts through the crowd. Someone breaks away, shouting and pointing as the effigy begins to flail its arms, and another scream echoes across the still waters—this time from the raft.

Forensic technician Moa Bakke and Detective Inspector Fredrik Dal are already on the scene—unwitting witnesses to one of the most gruesome crimes the once-peaceful islands have ever seen. In the days that follow, they'll be forced to question where their loyalties lie while the ghosts of the past refuse to stay buried.

Get your copy of *THE CLOVER*, which is available on Amazon.

THANKS

I want to thank my wonderful editor, Ashley Bartlett, who is a treasure.

A NOTE FROM THE AUTHOR

I hope you enjoyed this book and felt immersed in the Nordic Noir experience. I aim to create a small escape from the everyday world and knowing that my stories resonate with you means everything to me.

As a Scandinavian author, reaching a broader audience can be challenging; therefore, your support truly makes a difference. Your engagement as a reader inspires me to continue writing.

I'd love to hear your thoughts! If you enjoyed the book, please consider rating it, leaving a review, or recommending it to fellow readers. Your feedback helps me continue to craft stories that you'll enjoy. Thank you for being such a loyal reader.

Victoria
vmlarsson.com

ABOUT THE AUTHOR

VM Larsson, a Swedish author, is fascinated by how life shapes us into who we are, and she embraces the challenge of capturing the complexities of human nature in her writing.

To refine her craft, she immerses herself in textbooks and investigative reports while staying updated on the latest real-life drama in the news. Accurately portraying police procedures is essential for believability, but must also serve the story.

When she is not writing, you'll likely find her strolling along deserted beaches, where solitude sparks her imagination. It is perfect for dreaming up tales of serial killers and the heroes who bring them to justice.

Printed in Dunstable, United Kingdom

75233720R00134